EMIC RIZZLE,
TINKERER

MARY ANN DOMANSKA

MNEMOSYNE BOOKS
AN IMPRINT OF LETHE PRESS

Published by MNEMOSYNE BOOKS
An imprint of LETHE PRESS
118 Heritage Ave, Maple Shade, NJ 08052
lethepressbooks.com

ISBN 978-1-59021-777-1

Cover Art by
REIKO MURAKAMI

Cover and Interior Design by
INKSPIRAL DESIGN

To Clara & Andrew, ever my best source of inspiration,
and to my mom and dad, who let me believe that any dream is
possible.

Special thanks to Sandy, Ana-Maria, Mary, Lenny, Noël,
Steve Berman, and the late Dr. Georgia McWhinney.

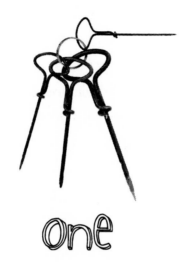

One

HER GRANDFATHER PLACED the old black journal on Emic's lap and said nothing. Her little hands moved across the tattered cover and lifted it open. She held back a sneeze as a musty smell floated off browned pages. On the inside cover was written "Nikola Tesla." Emic flipped through rough sketches—strange machines, diagrams, and mathematical equations. The pages were messy and smudged, some half torn out and others marked through feverishly in smears of black ink. Her grandfather told her, "Keep it safe, child. This book could change the world."

Emic squirmed in the oversized chair next to his

upright hospital bed with its bars and wires and remote controls. She put the heavy book into her pink Hello Kitty! backpack. "I promise, Grandpa."

He patted her head and eased back into his pillow. "Now let's play another game of War, shall we?" A cough began deep in his chest. Emic poured him a glass of water and gently put the plastic cup into his trembling hand.

"They will want to take it from you," he said after a long drink.

"Who are *they*?" She kept her voice a whisper as if someone might be eavesdropping on their conversation.

"The government." Sweat matted down her grandpa's silver hair in spots and spiked it up in others. She smoothed it neat as best she could. Grandpa had been in "the home," as her parents called it, for several years. Emic would take the school bus and get off there, even when she was in kindergarten. Her parents worked long hours, so she spent many afternoons with Grandpa, rearranging items on his windowsill, relocating a vase of flowers, putting his standup clock in a new spot, leaning books into different corners. She never tired of the stories he told. "Tell me about another great adventure where you saved someone's life, or jumped out of an airplane, or…" Emic would sit with her legs tucked up under her, bouncing and squealing, until the attendants popped their heads into the room. "Honey," (adults often called her

Honey or Sweetie, which irked her), "the other residents are resting. Shhh." But she knew Grandpa loved telling her stories: "Emily, would you like me to tell you about the time I saved a beautiful spy dangling from a tree after we parachuted into the South of France during World War II?"

"Are you tellin' the truth this time?" she always asked. "Or are you yanking me again, Colonel?"

"No, I'm not yanking your *chain*…this time. Or am I?"

Emic would lean in, squinting, and stare into his eyes. They would be nose-to-nose now, and both of them would start laughing. He'd then reach out and tickle her. "*Chère Emily! Ma petite tête de chou. Tu aimes jouer.*"

She had learned some French from him. "I do like to play. But I am not a little head of cabbage!" She giggled.

Gregor Rizzle spoke four languages besides English. This was because he had lived or worked in Russia, France, Germany, and Serbia. She knew that he was born in London, and that he was in France during World War II and had become a colonel. She also knew that Grandpa Gregor talked a lot about strange things, about a man named Tesla, a flying machine, and a secret power generator that needed no fuel for it to run. He called it "free energy."

"Oh, he's just going senile," her mother once said when Emic came home after a visit, when questions filled her mind and kept her from going to sleep. "He's only got a bunch of conspiracy theories left now, to keep his mind occupied. Now go to sleep."

"What's a conspiracy, Mother?" she would ask.

"You're a conspiracy! Now…Go. To. Sleep."

After her mother left the room, Emic, all tucked under her duvet, wiggled until she emerged from the warmth of her covers with a pocketknife in hand. She could never fall fast asleep when her head was so full of thoughts. Tinkering and art helped clear her head. So she set to work completing an etching; a portrait was carved of her grandfather on the lower righthand side of her wooden headboard. It showed the deep wrinkles of his forehead, the hollowness of his cheeks, the strength of his jawline, and his piercing eyes.

Grandpa had been all over the world. It was said that he could fix anything, sneak anywhere. Emic believed this was where she inherited her love of languages, of geography and history, and of taking things apart. Emic never wavered from her quest for discovery. She always planned methodically what she needed to do, whether it was to remove, take apart, alter, or create something. She also had her own collection of tools she could use in almost any situation. She especially loved the red Case double-X three-blade folding pocketknife her Grandpa had given her for her eighth birthday. It was the best present she ever got!

two

IT DID RAIN for the funeral.

"For those who don't know me, my name is Howard Rizzle. Thank you, everyone, for coming today. I can see my father touched a lot of lives. He was an unforgettable character, to say the least. First, he asked to have this poem read out loud to all of you who came here today. Emic?"

Emic stepped up to the dark wood podium and climbed the stool that had been set there for her. She unfolded the crinkly paper she had been clutching in her hand during the viewing part of the funeral service. Her father tilted the microphone down for her. She swallowed hard.

"I'll Be There." She sniffled as she admitted she hadn't been able to find the poem's author online.

There was no time to say goodbye
But this I ask—please do not cry
Remember me as you think best
The happy times—forget the rest.

Look for me and I'll be there
And you will find me everywhere
In the gentle touch of breeze
That cools the skin or swirls the leaves.

In the scent and color of flowers
That gave to me such happy hours
On sunny days under skies of blue
Just think of me, I'll be with you.

In winter when there's cloud or mist
The rain will give to you my kiss
As wood smoke lingers in the air
Look for me and I'll be there.

Where seagulls cry above the sea
And surf rolls in so endlessly
Among towering trees that soar above
In all these things that I once loved

Look for me and I'll be there
You'll feel my presence everywhere.

Emic stepped down from the stool and fell into her father's waiting arms. He could feel her need to cry, but taking a deep breath in and holding it tight in her lungs, she let him go so he could speak. She walked down the stairs, tears stubbornly streaming anyway, and sat down alone in the front pew of the church.

"Thank you, Emic. Now, I'd like to say a few words in memory of my father Gregor Rizzle. Some of you knew him as 'Colonel.' My father took great pride in being a veteran; being in the war so many years ago. Others knew him simply as Greg. To me he was 'Pops.' Pops certainly lived a remarkable life, one that inspired me greatly when I was a young man. His adventurous attitude, his broad range of abilities, and his tinkering spirit. I think he was more an inventor than a soldier. Pops was always working on some project out in the shed. But he was not a reclusive man. He always took a great interest in the people he met: there were few people he couldn't totally engage at any time or place, fascinating them with his knowledge of things and his passionate opinions of the world.

"My father pursued his many endeavors diligently, and always rose to meet a challenge. I always felt that he expected the same of me, too. He was a complicated man.

His expectations were high for himself and for all those around him. He had a tremendous sense of honor, loyalty, and truth. He was a master of criticism, too. With a few wry words, my father could be far more damning than most people could achieve with any strong language or loud voice. Well, though I can't fix anything without a manual to help me, I like to think I at least got my sense of humor from him.

"I'll miss the news of my father's many strange adventures, and I'll miss the stories from the seven continents he visited; I'll miss his many tales of World War II; about his old friends; and I'll even miss his many unbelievable conspiracy theories. Stories he told again and again, in the same exacting detail with every retelling. I'll also miss the surprising depth and scope of his knowledge. I will miss my father dearly and will forever wish I could have been a better son."

As EMIC AND her father rose to walk up the aisle at the end of the service, she could see the back left row was filled with four serious men in dark suits. They were muscular and clean-cut with very short hair, and they wore severe looks. The man at the end of the pew by the aisle seemed to be quickly taking a picture of them with his phone before tucking it into his inside breast pocket. The others filing out of the church clutched their hands, kissed their cheeks, patted their shoulders, and smeared away tears and mascara with crumpled tissues. Shortly after, the four odd men followed them out without saying a word or greeting anyone.

She wondered, *How did they know Grandpa?*

GRANDPA GREGOR DIED four years ago, just a month after Emic got that knife, his last gift to her. He had been her best friend for so long, and she often stopped to think about those visits. Emic's mom couldn't go to the funeral; she was in hospital having a baby. A boy, Brody. Grandpa Gregor never got to meet Brody.

After Grandpa Gregor died, subjects in school seemed to hold little meaning for Emic. They became frustrating, even boring. At times she would challenge her teachers or flat out disagree with them. At parent-teacher conferences, she overheard her teachers telling her parents that she was "precocious" and "obstinate."

In class, Emic could easily tune her teachers out by making plans for some grand robot that she would build someday, a robot that could be instructed to make beds, braid hair, or sew! It would even pick up Brody's toys that seemed to constantly be strewn around the house.

"Em, could you please pick up after Brody? I have to go to the grocery store?" or "Emily, those Legos need to go in the toy box before your father gets home. Do you mind helping?"

Most importantly, the robot's hands would become tools that could open anything. Emic kept detailed sketches of her grand robot in a large black wire-bound sketchbook she carried with her everywhere.

When Emic was in the sixth grade, the school Science department started a Robotics team. Mr. Harris, the science teacher who started the team and who happened to be Emic's favorite teacher, gave her the idea that she might just be able to put together that robot that had been in her head for so long. And she also realized that there were others like her, both girls and boys, who liked to make things work in different ways; liked to invent new things; liked to wonder *what if…?* So Emic joined the school Robotics team and at their first competition in the regional robotics league, they won first prize. Their game-playing creation was tested to meet the season's engineering challenges. It conquered every obstacle in the course, dunking balls in hoops, maneuvering through elaborate mazes, and executing every task with slow precision. Emic reveled in her team's success and she was no longer bored, no longer thought of as weird. Emic was smart. And her excitement for school returned.

EMIC WAS LIKE her father, Howard, in many ways. He was an architect, an artist and a visionary who preferred to work with pen and ink, but had recently lost his job. Apparently, his firm was looking for people with more technical skills, digital people. "Obsolete," Emic sometimes heard him moan in the days after losing his job.

It distressed Emic to see her father so deflated. He could not even muster a laugh at dinner, as she recounted how her latest creation had accidently escaped the robotics classroom, spun out into the hallway by the cafeteria, and tripped the school's principal, Mrs. Galloway. "Oh, how she howled as she lay there on her back!" laughed Emic. "The other teachers scurried around her like little ants, not sure what they should do. After a few minutes the school nurse helped Mrs. Galloway to her feet and she said she wasn't sure if she was hurt or not, but it seemed she was not. "How could you *not* know if you are hurt or not?" asked Emic. Brody howled like a wolf. At least that brought a slight smile to her father's face and he lifted Brody into the air and howled with him.

Emic did feel guilty about causing the accident, but really Mrs. Galloway was fine—it was Emic's little four-wheeled creature that had suffered far more damage than the principal, its back wheels dislocated and lost down the stairs somewhere, its axle snapped in half, its wires shredded and unusable. Emic glanced sadly at the mangled skeleton, now sitting on the mantle across from her, crushed by the weight of Mrs. Galloway!

"You are so much like your grandfather with all this robotics stuff," her father told her, his face lighting up for a moment. "Your understanding of things comes from touch, from building things. He too had to really get his hands on something, turn it over, twist it, break into it to understand it. Just like you, my little Tinkerer."

The big news came the next morning. It was Saturday, and Emic's mom, Sheila, was making cheesy-eggs and toast as the family gathered around the table for breakfast. Her parents were particularly quiet, and Emic had a feeling something was up. No one was even reading the newspaper—it sat still in its blue plastic bag by the back door. Even Brody was quietly playing, rolling his Play-Doh on the table, cookie cutters within reach.

This can't be good.

"How are you this morning?" her dad asked Sheila, then turning to Emic and Brody.

"Fine," Mom and Emic replied together. Brody didn't even look up. Her parents took turns glancing at each other, trying to figure out who would be the bad guy and break the news.

"Okay, what's goin' on?" Emic asked.

Mom spoke first. "We're going to move!"

"Where? Why? Wait…w-when?" stuttered Emic.

"I've been accepted into a post-graduate program at Lenoir-Rhyne University in North Carolina," Sheila said. "I can teach there part-time while working on my doctorate. Oh, it's a great opportunity for me, and Brody will get to join their pre-K program." She was clearly excited about these new possibilities opening up for them all.

"But," Emic said with a frown, "I've spent my whole life here in Chicago. What's in North Carolina for me?"

"We'll be living in a smaller town instead of the noisy city. It's called Flat Rock, in the foothills of the mountains. It's beautiful. Honest."

"Don't I have some say in this?" Emic was having a hard time adjusting to this rush of new information.

"Em, they've already found us a beautiful house. It's the strangest thing," she pondered. "Someone at the school called late last night to let us know we could start packing." Mom tried to smile while saying this, as she tried to make the news exciting for Em. "It has a wraparound porch— I've always wanted one of those—and a big backyard where we can plant a real garden."

"But I just started liking school here."

Brody, not wanting to be left out of the conversation, chimed in, "I want to be in the *gadget* program, Mommy".

"Em, I can't refuse this chance. I have to follow the work. Times are hard, and we can't get by here anymore since your dad's been laid off from his firm." Her mother stroked Brody's cheek. "And you, my little man, can start in the gadget program and work your way up to the graduate program."

Emic noticed that her mother's voice sounded light and happy but she looked worried. Frown lines on the forehead were a giveaway.

Emic had lost her appetite. She saw her father's sad face, and not wanting to make things worse, she started to clean up the dishes from the table. "A wraparound porch, huh?" she said. Emic blurted out: "Zucchini!"

"I think we should plant some tomatoes, what do you think?" her father added, "and basil, of course." This was a game they played when things looked bleak: imagining a magnificent vegetable garden. One trellised and fenced by Emic's tinkering, of course.

"Onions, too," her mother said.

"Yuk" came from Brody.

Her father began sketching the garden on the morning newspaper. "Sheila, don't you think it's a bit odd they're renting a house for us? Do schools normally do that for students in their fellowship program?"

"Maybe I really impressed them with my latest article? Stop worrying! Be proud of my success and let's just be grateful for this opportunity."

Emic could tell by her father's expression that he did not trust this good fortune as easily as Mom did. Or Emic herself.

three

EMIC EASED OFF the curb with a *plunk,* as the wooden basket on the back of her bike rattled against the metal frame. Her bicycle was no ordinary BMX from Walmart. Originally, the twenty-inch "Kent 2 Cool" Girl's BMX Bike that she assembled with help from her dad came in a shade called Pink Satin Rose. That could not last long. She quickly rummaged through her paint supplies (mainly half-used cans of outdoor house paint that had been discarded and then retrieved) and came across a dark blue-gray color called Slate. The almost-black hue seemed much less girly, and Emic couldn't wait to slather it over the swirly designs.

Normally, Emic would not have been able to bike to school in Chicago in December with its biting cold winds but a strange winter Chinook, as her dad called it, had taken hold and temperatures had been strangely spring-like for the last week. It was still chilly and dark as the sun had not quite risen.

Swerving to avoid a pothole in the road, Emic noticed a squirrel darting out from the sidewalk and attempting to cross the busy two-lane street before her. She squeezed her horn to warn him, and the quiet of the street erupted with the noise of a blaring siren. The bewildered squirrel scurried back onto the sidewalk and into the neighbor's overgrown hedges. A car traveling on the road contained a man who was equally alarmed by the loud and unexpected noise that came from her small bicycle. Just as suddenly as the squirrel leaping for its life, the unsuspecting driver swerved in the opposite direction, crossed the empty oncoming lane, launched over a small embankment, mowed through several piles of leaves that had been recently heaped into large mounds, and shuddered to an abrupt stop.

Emic shouted an apology as she steadied her handlebars, feeling more sorry for the little squirrel than she did for the man, who was now thrashing his arms angrily out of the window of his old brown car. "I think I need to make a slight adjustment to the audio output," she said to herself, eyeing the cables and wires that connected a small iPod to a speaker that was rigged to her horn. *But not today.* Today Emic needed the iPod set just as loud as possible.

Turning into the parking lot of the brick-built school building, Emic could feel her fingers tighten around the black knobby handle-grips. A small group, composed of boys who seemed intent on finding ways to cause Emic's cheeks to flush, palms to sweat, and forehead to wrinkle, had gathered along the pathway that led to the only bike rack near the middle school, with three or four of them on either side. She pressed on the foot-brake, lifting herself off the seat into an almost standing position as she pumped the pedals and approached. She had upped the volume on the speaker just for them, just for this moment, but now she hesitated, thumb poised to initiate the blare, imagining them scattering and screaming. Emic's heart was beating fast, but she was not feeling flustered or nervous now. No, Emic was feeling exhilarated, empowered, but...

Just as Emic was about to press down on the button, Mr. Caldwell, the tall, lanky assistant principal, seemed to appear out of nowhere. He was a black man with large, black-rimmed glasses, wearing a trim charcoal-gray suit and a gleaming sideways smile. He started shooing the boys towards the school building and followed them up the stairs. Emic coasted to the bike rack, relieved that her arrival had passed without serious incident today, but with her knuckles still white when she finally let go. She chained her rattling creation to the bars, letting out a long steady breath through her pursed lips. Emic thought she saw Mr. Caldwell glance back over his shoulder, and smile even more broadly at her.

As THE FINAL school bell rang and the heavy metal doors flung open at the end of the day, Emic raced down the steps two at a time. She could see something was wrong as soon as she hit the bottom step. Her bike was still there, but the tires were completely flat and her basket was gone. It had taken Emic three days to make her basket, using her favorite colors of green and purple. Using rope and yarn, she had woven a warp-wrap rope basket with a pattern of alternating green and purple bands. Emic bit her lip hard as her face turned red. She closed her eyes for a moment, and when she opened them, standing next to her shoulder to shoulder was Luna, wrapping her slender arm around Emic.

Emic gave her best friend a subtle silent nod, and then bent down to unchain her bike. "Hey, my grandma can give you a ride home—we can throw your bike in the back," Luna said in a comforting tone.

"No, it's okay—it's not too far," Emic mumbled. "...

Besides, your house is in the other direction," she added
with a shrug of her shoulders. "Anyway, don't you have an
ice-skating lesson?"

Luna nodded.

As Luna walked away, Emic continued: "Really, I'm
fine…" Emic's voice was determined, and Luna knew her
well enough not to argue, so she just shrugged.

"Those boys are just…ghouls." Emic was trying to
think of other names for people who behaved so badly,
when she was brought back from her daydreaming by
Luna, who turned, and with a mystified look shouted:
"Hey, where's your basket?"

"Dunno. I can make another one. I guess I'll have to
find a way to lock it on."

Luna, her eyebrows raised, whispered in a hushed tone
that indicated conspiracy, "Or you could booby-trap it."

A light came on in Emic's eyes as the possibilities
rushed in. That did not seem like a terrible idea at all.

As Emic heaved the front tire over the curb in front of
their house, she looked up just in time to see the curtain
in the front-room window being yanked down. "Oh no."
She dropped the bike right there on the front lawn and
ran toward the front door. She fumbled for her door key
that was connected to her belt on a self-winding pulley-
cord, then, realizing that the door was already open,

almost fell head over heels through the door way. Emic was then presented with the unfortunate result of her tardiness: Brody was home. Her little brother's school bus had arrived before her and she knew he must have been home for at least twenty minutes. This was bad. This was really, really bad. Since he started pre-kindergarten, it had been her job to meet him every day at the bus stop, bring him into the house, give him a healthy snack, and keep the little four year old entertained until their mother got home around four o'clock. Today, because she had to push her bike the eight blocks to home, that obviously did not happen. Brody had been smart enough to let himself in, and quiet enough that their dad hadn't come down from his study. Instead of finding everything in order, her mother was going to find a box of grape juice tipped over and pouring out of the open refrigerator onto the kitchen floor, and a trail of chocolate chip cookies and crumbs leading into the living room. Emic could see her great aunt's colorful, antique, patchwork-quilt-patterned teddy bear cookie jar. It lay cracked in pieces on the tiled floor. The window drapes had been yanked down and were now covering the coffee table. And standing beside the coffee table, with chocolate drool running down his face, was little Brody, contemplating a cut on his finger. Mom was *not* going to be happy. Emic knew she should have been home sooner. She was certain it was the boys that let the air out of her tires, and she resolved that tomorrow she'd set the volume on her speaker to full blast.

"Brody, I am in so much trouble. Hey, what happened to the curtains?" Judging by the disheveled state of the throw pillows, her little brother must have been jumping on the couch, lost his balance and grabbed onto the curtains as he fell. Emic scooped up the remaining package of cookies, as Brody grinned up at her with a mouth full of brown teeth. She couldn't help but smile a bit at the predicament.

"I told you mom bought 'em for me," Brody sang in a taunting voice.

"But you're not supposed to eat them all at once, Bro. Come on. Let's get you cleaned up before mom gets home. Do you want some milk to wash that down?"

"Okay. Can you make it chocolate?"

"Sure, why not?" she said. *Healthy snack, not today,* she thought.

As Emic was busy sopping up the purple grape juice off the floor, half a roll of paper towels in hand, she could hear her mother fumbling with the keys in the door. Brody jumped up, and predictably knocked over the full glass of thick, dark chocolate milk, soaking his t-shirt and pants and creating a puddle beneath him on the cream-colored carpet. Emic stood up and readied herself for the lecture that was to follow.

"You have *one* responsibility, Em. Just one. I need to trust you. I depend on you to come straight home after school. Were you late again? What were you doing this time? Did you go back to that old junkyard for more parts? We've talked about this. You know Brody can't be left alone. Oh, my cookie jar! It can't be replaced, you know that. Your Great Aunt Dot made that cookie jar. You should have called your dad to let him know. What were you thinking?"

Emic's mother knelt down and scooped up several larger pieces of the shattered ceramic cookie jar. A sloshing noise, and the sound of wet denim rubbing together, indicated Brody was approaching them from behind.

"Look at you, sweetie. You're a mess. Em, spray down that carpet so it doesn't stain, will you? I'm going to put him in the bathtub. I'll be back to help in a minute. But this can't happen again. How can we make sure this doesn't ever happen again?"

Emic kept quiet and continued to soak up the grape juice with paper towels. She vaguely listened to the lecture as it continued, even as her mother ascended the staircase with her brother on her hip. Her mother's voice could still be heard as she trotted down the hallway, finally fading away as the bathroom door clicked closed and the bath water started to run.

Emic took a neglected cookie that had been left

behind on the counter, savoring it as she walked over and started to spray foamy cleaner onto the mud-colored mess on the carpet.

four

EMIC SHOULD HAVE been packing. Instead, she pulled out her toolkit from underneath the bed. She had an extensive array of tools now, including scissors, wire cutters, and a screwdriver she'd borrowed from her father so many years ago. Opening the lid and lifting up the top drawer, she pulled out the black journal. She flipped it open to a bookmarked page with a small blueprint of a contraption. Next, she slid out a cardboard box from underneath her bed. Inside was a small device based on the plan on the page. Emic studied the messy text and attempted to translate the words into meaning. She was spread out on the floor, surrounded by copper colored magnet wire, insulated wire, aluminum sheets, plastic transparency sheets, and the twelve-volt battery she had borrowed from Brody's battery-powered ride-on tyke's jeep. She poured her frustration into the machine, adamant to make it work and to figure out what it could do. It began to click and whir and then the black and red wires attached to her homemade power source sparked and died with a popping flash. The plastic part of the capacitor melted right to the wooden base of her prototype. Her temper flared and she threw her screwdriver across the room, impaling it into the wall above her bed. Then she carefully laid the unlit light bulb back in the box.

Emic still couldn't believe it. She would be leaving her school over winter break and wouldn't return to finish her sixth grade year. Mostly she was afraid of how she would ever make another friend like Luna. Luna had moved to Chicago the year before. She was from Winnipeg, Canada. Boisterous, unafraid, always speaking out of turn, Luna loved to find reasons to laugh and make others laugh. Emic didn't know what to think of her at first. It was as if she had found her opposite. Some of their classmates jokingly called them Yin and Yang, and it stuck.

Emic had always been quiet, more willing to work on a project or look up something in a book than to start up a conversation or game at recess. Before Luna, Emic often would have found herself in the computer lab during lunch recess, working on a new design for the 3-D printer, while others would be planning out performances or dancing on the bleachers for their friends at the end of the playing field. But one day during her fifth grade year, after there had been a lot of rain, the roof collected so much water that it partially collapsed into the lab and destroyed many of the computers, effectively closing the computer lab for the remainder of the school year. So, forced outside, she brought her sketchbook, propped herself up against a tree by the fence along the woods, and imagined what she would, or hoped she would, be doing when summer came.

Suddenly, an orange rubber kickball came crashing down on top of her sketchbook, sending her pencil flying out of her hand. Looking up, sun blinding her at first, she saw a girl with long, dark blond, wavy hair. The wind that day had whipped her hair up so that she looked like a witch, or maybe a wild fairy, hovering above her.

"Hey," Emic cried out, noticing the dirt that had streaked across her paper.

"I'm sorry. I saw the ball coming at you from over there," she said, waving her hand, "so I ran towards you to try and stop it from hitting you. I guess I just wasn't fast enough. I called out heads up but you must not have heard me. Are you okay?"

"Oh, thanks. Yeah, I'm fine," Emic sighed as she

searched around for her charcoal pencil.

Luna saw it in a bush nearby, retrieved it, and handed it, eraser first, back to Emic. "I'm Luna Federico," she said. "I just started school this year. I'm in Ms. Everett's class. Aren't you in 5K with Mr. Kinney?"

"Yeah," Emic offered but no more.

"What were you drawing? Can I see it?"

Biting her bottom lip, thinking how she might escape from sharing her plan but seeing no way, Emic reluctantly flipped open her book to the last drawing. It was an elaborate tree house that she wanted to build with her father in the summer.

"We have the most perfect, wide-spreading old beech tree just at the edge of our backyard. My dad and I have been talking about starting this tree house project for a couple of years now." He had even begun teaching her how to make simple architectural sketches, and was letting her use his special grid paper and black ink drawing pens from his work. He had tacked up some of the designs they'd made in his study, near his slanted drawing table. In the shed, he had begun collecting the necessary two-by-fours, a bright green split-door he'd found in the trash on his way home from work, a window frame complete with double-paned glass, and a wooden fence segment that would serve as a railing for the little side porch.

"What? Wow! I've never seen anything like it? That

is a tree house? That's marvelous!" Luna was obviously impressed and plopped down uninvited next to Emic. Luna pulled together her wild hair, tying it into a messy knot at the back. Emic could see all thoughts of recovering the ball were now forgotten as it bounced over the fence and into the woods behind the schoolyard.

That afternoon at recess, as the other girls and boys whizzed around them in a blur, Emic and Luna sat by the big oak tree and talked about outlandish tree houses with skylights, running water, and pulley systems connecting to their kitchens so that their moms could just send dinner up to them. Luna also shared how she'd moved to Chicago with her mom and little brother when her parents divorced. Her father stayed in Canada, remarried, and was beginning a new family, but her mom was now sick, so they were living with their grandparents for a little while.

That was the afternoon they became the best of friends. The move, Emic was afraid, would ruin everything! None of the other girls thought her designs were cool! None of the other girls made her laugh, or taught her how to braid her long hair. None of the other girls were Luna, and she was sure she wouldn't meet anyone else like her!

Change was coming. Things would never be the same. Thinking of Luna, thinking of her tree house, thinking of leaving her robotics team, Emic stood facing the mirror in her bathroom. Pulling around the long braid that Luna had so delicately weaved for her at school, admiring its tight smoothness, she reached for her scissors. Snip!

five

THE BOXES WERE stacked everywhere. Her mother had given her a big black Sharpie to label her boxes: EMIC'S TOYS, EMIC'S CLOTHES, and the largest box, EMIC'S TOOLS. She woke up super early on the morning the movers were coming. She trudged around the house, staring at the bare walls where paintings had hung, noticing how the deeper brown colors of the wood floors had been protected from years of sunlight under rugs— rugs now rolled, tied, leaning against the walls and waiting for removal. The surrounding floorboards were bleached a faded orange color. She roamed from room to room: the kitchen with its bare cupboards and cabinet doors left wide open; the living room stark and empty except for a few red ribbon bows scattered on the deep mauve carpet, left over from hastily opened Christmas presents three days before; the library, whose shelves were empty, dusty, and without purpose.

Turning to leave the library, she noticed that one of the boxes was labeled GRANDPA GREGOR. She stood frozen in her spot, tilting her head to the side in curiosity. She still deeply missed her grandfather—their connection, their friendship, lingered for her in ways she could not articulate. No one had mentioned his name in months. Her father, she knew, believed he had turned into a crazy old man with even crazier ideas.

The box was securely taped, but that never stopped Emic when she wanted to get into something. She returned with her Case pocketknife, easily slicing through the packing tape and popping open the side of the box (easier to hide the damage there, less noticeable). Kneeling over the contents of the box with great intent, she carefully lifted out the top stack of papers, certificates, letters, and photographs. Next came an old wooden cigar box. On it was printed, "5¢ YELLOW CAB *Extremely Mild* Quality Style." "PANATELA" was etched in bold, burnt-colored letters vertically along the right side. The latch at the front of the soft brown box was a rusty brass color and it slid open stiffly to the left, away from the hook closure. It still had the faint smell of cigars or smoke as she peeled back its lid. Emic gasped! Inside was the smaller box that Emic remembered Grandpa Gregor had taken the medal out of when he showed it to her. It was a long, narrow blue box. Its case felt like velvet. When she opened the lid, she noticed that it was hinged and snapped closed when the lid was lowered. Inside, the box was covered in a gold textured cloth that felt like brittle felt.

There was a sudden flash of excitement on Emic's face. She felt something shift inside the cigar box. Shaking it, she heard something rattle. Emic quickly found a letter opener and popped out a molded, fabric-covered medal holder. Underneath it, she found a man's gold ring. Standing upright at the back were a few postcards with faded pencil in fanciful cursive scribbling on the back.

Emic heard the deep rumbling of a large truck driving up their street, causing the windowpanes to rattle a little. She knew it was the movers. She put down everything and ran over to the curtain-less window. Swirls of ice had made imprints on the glass pane, like cut paper snowflakes. Branches by her bedroom window dangled with icicles, dripping from the warming winter sun. "J.J. & Sons" was printed on the side of the mustard-colored truck in bright red lettering. There was an illustration of three jolly men, arm in arm, smiling goofy grins, the two younger ones on either side clutching boxes under their strong bulky arms. She imagined the depiction was playing off of the idea of performers in an old-timey circus. All that was missing seemed to be the elephant and the high-wire walker.

Stealthily replacing the papers, then resealing the box along its side by putting a fresh piece of tape over the damaged part, Emic quickly concealed her crime. She tucked the cigar box under her left arm and bounced up the stairs to her room, skipping the steps that she knew would creak. She had just ducked into her room when her father finished showering and the bathroom door opened. Her mother was getting ready to come down to greet the movers and begin the long day's work ahead. Brody was happily climbing in and out of the few remaining empty boxes. One minute the boxes were a train engine and caboose, and the next minute he was stacking all the boxes and building a skyscraper. It was not difficult to know his whereabouts with the loud sirens coming from his new fire truck. Unlike Emic, Brody Wan Kenobi left the batteries in his toys.

"Time to evacuate the premises," her father called at Emic's door a moment later, trying to make light of the situation. He always liked to joke and had an unusual sense of humor. They called it "Howard humor."

Emic let out a sigh. She took the small box from under her arm and slipped it into her pillowcase, then folded her pillow in half. They would be bagging up her bedclothes soon and breaking down her bed to transport it exactly 641 miles away.

It was blustery cold outside. It had snowed a full foot the week before and she knew the wind would be biting at her nose and ears. The doorbell chimed and she could hear the familiar creaking as her mother went down the stairs to meet the moving men. She greeted them and offered to make them a pot of coffee. That was her mother's way with strangers—Sheila worked hard to make people feel welcome and comfortable. She was already making plans for a guest room in North Carolina so their friends and family could visit once things had settled down. She had purchased a large can of paint marked "Robin's Egg Blue" so she could start painting once they moved in. Her mother liked pretty things, so the guests would be greeted by the sunny yellow, pale blue, and soft pink-flowered quilt her sister, Birdie, had made by hand and given to Sheila and Howard as a wedding gift. There would be white doilies that were handmade by her grandmother, Dolores, on the side table beneath a lamp, and a vase she would fill with fresh-cut flowers to greet her house guests. Her mother collected friends the way other people collected stamps.

"Sheila! Everything's so beautiful," they would say as they put their overnight bags or suitcases down on the antique luggage rack and moved around the room admiring how welcoming it was. Emic imagined her mother leaving little things on their pillows, like mints in a fancy hotel.

Thinking of friends made Emic think of Luna. She reached for her new cell phone and sent her friend a text:

The movers r here. Coming over?

The chime came from Luna a moment later.

Of course! What time?

Emic thought maybe Luna was still in bed. It was only about 7:40 AM and she knew her friend was not an early riser on the weekends. Luna's room was full of comfortable things: an oversized plush hot-pink beanbag chair that would have taken up almost half the width of Emic's room, the fluffiest down comforter she'd ever seen on a very high four-poster bed. It was much more girly than Emic would have liked, but it was comfortable. When they had sleepovers at Luna's grandparents' house, Luna would just share the bed with her friend, it was so big.

How about 4? we still have a lot of packin to do, Emic typed.

Then she added, *We're leaving at 5.* She felt her throat tighten at the thought of it. She imagined it would be like some sad movie, straining her neck to look back at her childhood home growing smaller in the distance. She closed her eyes and willed herself to pull it together, pressing her lips tightly together, determined not to cry.

OK came the message back in an instant.

Her stomach twisted in knots as she dressed, knowing this would be her last outfit, her last day, her last everything in this house she had grown up in.

The day passed quickly. The burly men, who looked nothing like the lean young men portrayed on the truck, worked at a steady pace, hauling out the bigger pieces of furniture first, then carrying box after box out to the sidewalk. In reality, the movers were stocky and a bit round at the middle. It was obvious they were related, but she didn't see the "J.J." or father figure among them.

Maybe they acquired a cousin and the sons decided to let their father rest, she thought.

The front door was left wide open, letting gusts of winter chill the house. The movers didn't bother closing it behind them with each trip and no one could be bothered to follow them and close it every time, so everyone was wearing coats inside the house.

Emic ventured one last time up to her tree house. It was bitter cold. She could see her own breath as she made her way up through the trap door. She sat in the bare little room on the floor planks, shivering, remembering her afternoons there with Luna. They had painted the inside of it together in a mural of beach scenes, deep space, and pyramids in Egypt. They had nailed up shelves and boxes to hold all their many treasures. It was a clubhouse built for two.

As the house emptied, room by room, she realized Luna would be arriving soon. "Mama, where's my present for Luna?" she called, coming into the house almost panicked, afraid it might have accidently been picked up along with everything else, and lost somewhere among the piles of boxes stacked tightly inside the truck.

"Check the kitchen counter. I put a note on it so the movers would know not to take it. It's there, honey." Sheila called a lot of people "honey." She'd grown up in North Carolina, so for her, returning would feel a bit like going home. Emic knew *she* would not blend in so easily. Emic had always lived in the suburbs of Chicago.

Emic's gift for Luna was neatly wrapped in recycled comic strip pages from the Sunday paper. It even had a homemade bow made of leftover brown wrapping paper. She was relieved to have it ready.

"Emic! Emic, where are you?"

Luna bounded through the front door dragging Sol behind her.

Luna's mom, Carol, bellowed, "It's freezing!" as she smiled at her friend Sheila. Luna's and Emic's mothers had become friends too. They had the boys, Brody and Sol, at nearly the same age. As the girls grew closer, their time together increased and there were the inevitable phone calls to find out which parent was dropping off and which parent was bringing home from play dates. Some days the two women sat together and had coffee with vanilla almond milk or tea and biscuits while the boys entertained one another. Luna's mom had dropped off her coffee pot stating matter-of-factly, "The last thing you'll want to do before taking off is fill your thermos, especially in this weather," and now she would take the coffee pot home.

Emic could hear Brody and Sol clicking together Lego pieces in the hallway and chattering. One of Brody's Christmas presents was the *Star Wars* Snowspeeder and he was flying it over the banister railing and crashing into a Stormtrooper held by Sol. Content and occupied, she knew they still had a few minutes before someone would shout "Time to go."

"Let's go up to my room," Emic suggested to Luna. She'd left her own door closed, hoping it might stay a few degrees warmer in there. They stepped over the abandoned, scattered Lego pieces cluttering the hallway on the second floor.

"It looks so empty," Luna commented as they walked through the house.

"Yeah." Emic wasn't sure how to respond. "Come on. I want to show you something."

As soon as the door was closed, Emic unwrapped her

pillow, which she wanted to take with her on the long car ride south. She produced the little wooden box and held its contents out for Luna to see. They examined the medal and each postcard.

"Who's Hélène?" Luna asked.

"What?"

"The postcards. The postcards to your grandfather. They're from someone named Hélène?"

Emic hadn't really had the time to read them. She assumed they were from family and friends.

"I don't know. My grandmother's name was Zelda."

"Em, honey, come down with the last of your stuff. We need to pack up the car now and I need you to help me with Brody. It's almost time to go. We want to make it to your cousin's house by bedtime," her mother called through the door. A look came across Emic's face as if to say, "Ugh."

"What's the matter?" Luna asked.

"We're staying with my Aunt Birdie and Uncle Ray in Maryland tonight for a short visit and then driving on to our new house tomorrow. My cousin, Jacob, is such a pain. He's always making fun of me."

"Well, not this time!" Luna said. "I've got an idea. You need to…"

THEY DISCUSSED WHAT Emic should do as her parents hauled the last of their belongings to the car.

"Emily!" her mother called again, this time from the bottom of the stairs.

Then she remembered the present. Emic quickly produced her handmade gift. Inside was a bouquet of brightly colored paper flowers. When she moved over a paperclip with her thumb to touch a coin cell battery, the flower centers all opened and began to brightly glow.

"How did you do that?"

"Just some paper circuits and a little conductive tape," Emic answered.

Luna, in turn, brought out a small box from her coat pocket. Emic unwrapped layer after layer of colorful protective tissue paper until she finally reached the woven friendship bracelet tucked inside.

"I made it for you. They're your favorite colors, right? Purple and green?"

"I love it, Luna. I'll wear it until it falls off and then I'll re-tie it again."

They hugged, sitting there on the bare, cold floor in the empty room. And Emic knew they were out of time. She gathered up her grandfather's things and wrapped the box back up in her pillowcase. The friends looked around her room and said nothing else.

Emic had been dreading a cheesy scene, like from

the movies. But as she craned her neck from the back car window to wave goodbye to her friend, Emic refused to cry. With her other hand, she gripped the box hidden beneath her pillow. She tried to think about the mystery that had come out of nowhere. She decided she would do some digging and find out more about this Hélène. But how could she get at the truth without giving herself away? She couldn't just blurt out, "Who is Hélène?" to her father—he'd know that she'd been rooting around in his things. They had a great trust in each other. She didn't want him to know that she had taken something. No, she'd have to do this on her own.

six

WHEN THEY ARRIVED at her aunt and uncle's house, Emic's neck hurt from resting against one of the suitcases all those hours. Brody must have been really good, entertaining himself with his Etch A Sketch, cheddar cheese crackers and toys in a bag that Howard had put together for the journey. It was well after eleven o'clock at night, but her aunt let out a ridiculously loud scream anyway, and ran up the driveway to hug Sheila.

"Let's get you inside. Jacob... Jacob! Come out and grab some of those bags and help out, for goodness sakes," her aunt hollered. Jacob lumbered out. They had all stayed up to greet them. Knowing Jacob, he'd probably been engrossed in some stupid, violent video game. He was fourteen, stocky, and smelled of sweet musky cologne.

He must douse himself in it every morning.

Begrudgingly Jacob lifted two of the smallest bags he came across in the trunk. Emic remembered the advice Luna had given her and smirked.

Within minutes, Emic was on a lumpy futon bed in a room even smaller than the one she'd left behind. There were crates of old magazines, cleaning supplies, and piles of old clothes everywhere. They might be sisters, but her mother and Aunt Birdie (short for Beatrice) had very different ideas about hosting guests.

Made it. Goodnight, she texted Luna, knowing it was probably too late but still hoping for some response from her friend.

good ur safe miss u already, she got a moment later.

miss u too, Emic sent and soon fell asleep.

IN THE MORNING she could smell bacon and pancakes. There were pots banging and a dog barking somewhere outside. Her aunt's dog—a big black lab named Muscoe—hobbled up the half-level to Emic's tiny storage room, nosed the door open and slobbered all over her face with his big tongue.

Emic smiled, and wiped her face with her blanket,

reaching out her arm to pet this silly, wagging creature standing over her. His whole body seemed to be vibrating with anticipation. She wished she'd had a pet. Maybe at their new house, she thought. Emic dressed quickly and went downstairs. There was Brody Wan Kenobi still in his Star Wars pajamas. Part of the daily newspaper was rolled in his hand imitating a light saber. Poor Muscoe didn't seem too keen on getting close to the rolled-up newspaper. And Brody Wan didn't look too keen on getting his face licked.

Breakfast was a buffet, with everything you could imagine seeing at a large country-style restaurant! There were eggs (your choice of scrambled or fried), French toast spread out on a platter, homemade blueberry pancakes, several varieties of bagels with lox and cream cheese, crispy bacon, some odd-looking meat cut into neat squares, and a big pitcher of fresh orange juice at the center of the table.

Her cousin was already working greedily on a plate with some of everything on it. He didn't even pause to look up when his mother entered the room. Brody had blueberry stains and syrup on his chin and was happily crunching on some crispy bacon.

"Honey, get yourself a plate and dig in! Sheila, coffee's on!" Aunt Birdie called as she came through the doorway.

"Aunt Birdie, what's that?" Emic asked pointing to the thin slabs of dark brown meat.

"Darlin', *that* is livermush. It's the best darned fried stuff you'll ever eat."

Emic quickly tucked her phone down by her lap and looked up "livermush." According to Wikipedia: "Livermush is a Southern United States food product composed of pig liver, head parts, and cornmeal. It is commonly spiced with pepper and sage." She decided to give it a try anyway and found it was pretty tasty.

Emic knew her parents were anxious to get to their new home and begin the arduous process of unpacking, and her mom had to start her new job on Monday and this was Saturday. Emic's new school would have already been back in session for a week after the winter break. If she was still in Chicago she'd be entering the sixth grade, the final year of elementary. Now she would be going to a middle school that started with grade six, so instead of being among the oldest students, she would be among the youngest.

Would she be lucky enough to have a teacher like Mr. Harris? Would they have a computer lab? Would her new classmates just think she was weird? Emic knew for sure that they would not be able to understand her name. It was a nickname she'd acquired long ago. Her full name was Emily Michael Rizzle. The Michael was after her mother's father, Michael, who had been a well-loved preacher at a Baptist church in her mother's hometown of

Hendersonville, North Carolina. Emily never seemed to suit her and she desperately wanted a nickname like some of her classmates. Her father had suggested Emic and it seemed to stick, though her mother never called her that. Em, sometimes, but usually it was just Emily.

Emic knew her style would stand out, too. Her hair was spiky, almost iridescent black. It was thick and easy to take care of because of its new short 1920s length. Emic loved not having to fix her hair! She also had a taste for mismatched clothes, or clothes from different eras. She especially loved the blue leather wingtip Oxfords that her dad had helped her find on eBay for her twelfth birthday. She loved wearing long skirts made out of recycled sweaters or old ties. She'd sewn together a few, herself, using her mother's sewing machine. Even the reading glasses that she sometimes wore made her appear like she was from another time. They were sparkly green cat-eye styled frames that she'd picked up from a yard sale, and her mom had them replace the lenses for her.

Jacob looked up at Emic when his mother offered her a glass of orange juice. "I want some!" Pancake fell out of the sides of his mouth. She poured them each a glass and everyone sat down. Muscoe sat wagging his tail, weight moving from paw to paw. Papa leaned in and went nose to nose with Brody, setting Brody's plate in front of him and asking: "Syrup, honey or jam on the pancakes?"

Brody lifted a sausage from the plate and tried to answer while simultaneously taking a bite of his sausage. Muscoe seemed to know that little boys might drop their sausage if startled. He gave a loud "woof" and, apparently delighted with the result, lifted himself off the floor and spun around before lapping up the sausage. Brody knocked over his orange juice and Howard went to get something to clean up the mess.

"Oh, Birdie, it is nice to see you. I wish we could have visited for longer, but I just have to get things organized for next week so I'm ready to start my new job."

Her father came back over to the table just then with a dishtowel, catching the end of the conversation. He frowned. Emic was reminded that he had to start looking for a job and, until he found one, things would be tight. Emic resolved to need nothing and ask for nothing. Maybe she would even find a little job in her new neighborhood to help out. She could walk dogs or be a mother's helper, she thought.

"That's all right. I'm just glad you and Howard, Emic and Brody could stay over, and now you're a whole lot closer than before so you'll just have to come right on back up here once things get settled," her aunt announced with a slight southern accent.

Everyone ate too much. After breakfast, Howard and her Uncle Chuck went outside to begin packing up the car to leave, while the women busied themselves with cleaning the table and putting dishes in the dishwasher, chatting about the move and other boring things.

Jacob threw a small blueberry muffin across the table onto Emic's plate. "Eat this! You're so skinny you look like a skeleton. What are you, *anorexic*? You look like a twig or somethin'? And what's up with that red scarf tied around your head? It's like somethin' out of the fifties."

Emic smiled, remembering that part of Luna's advice was to "stay calm, cool, and collected." Oh, and did she ever!

"Jacob, it would be so nice if you grew up. And just so you are aware, that cologne…it doesn't make you smell any better."

As she continued, Aunt Birdie came back over to the table. "And thank you, Jacob, for noticing my scarf. I like it, too."

"Were you giving your cousin a compliment? Oh Jacob, I'm so proud of you. She is such a pretty girl, isn't she? I'm glad the two of you are getting along so well."

Jacob sat there stunned, utterly unable to respond. How could he make a comeback after that? Emic knew she had won that round.

Aunt Birdie was holding a birthday-party-type bag with a small rope handle, which she shoved towards Emic in such a matter-of-fact way that it was clear she expected Emic to accept her gift. Inside was a complete DVD collection of Star Wars. It was not new. Aunt Birdie giggled as she explained, "Emic, you can show Brody Wan Kenobi where he got his nickname".

As they left, Emic decided to text Luna about the encounter at breakfast. *Good advice,* she sent.

Awesome! glad to help, was the response and suddenly the miles didn't seem so far between them. Emic smiled and settled into her pillow again, watching the trees and the signs and the occasional cow pass by.

"Moo!" they would all sing each time they saw one. It was a leftover childhood game. The next thing she knew, the car was slowing and turning and stopping. They had arrived.

The yellow house seemed much bigger than the pictures she'd seen. It was also much older than her old house—a three-story twin—in Chicago. The white paint on the big wraparound porch was peeling and a white porch swing lay broken by the railing.

"Well, looks like I'll have some things to fill my time," her father said, trying to appear cheerful as they began unloading the car. The movers would not arrive until that afternoon, so everyone had time to explore. Her mother put her hand on Emic's shoulder.

"Do you want to see your room, sweetie?"

It was on the third floor—the entire length of it! It was a converted attic space and it was huge! The roof leaned on either side with high exposed beams, with a large, round window at each end. She knew why her father had liked this old farmhouse. It was full of character, with its deep windowsills, high ceilings and openness. There were doors everywhere. There was even a small door, about half her own height, on one side of her room. She opened it, and inside was a long storage space that must have been added when the attic was converted to a living space. It would be perfect for a workroom, with its built-in shelves and dark cedar wood lining.

Emic began bringing up her many boxes and bags from the car, tacking up her favorite sketches. She put the cigar box in the farthest dark corner of her new workroom behind her wingtip Oxfords shoebox. She resolved to wait until that night to read over the postcards. She also resolved to further investigate the remaining contents of that cardboard box labeled "GRANDPA GREGOR." What else would she find? She burned with curiosity. She knew he was in the military. She knew he had graduated from West Point in 1934. She knew he became a colonel. But she also knew that something had happened that no one was willing or able to talk about. What other clues were there?

THE RUMBLING OF the big truck returned, and Emic

knew their movers had arrived. Again at her window, a very different window, she peered out at the street below and saw the circus coming to town. Out stepped the first performer, still clutching a gooey half-eaten cheeseburger. Obviously they'd made a pit stop at a drive-thru on the way into town. This time an older man was with them.

That must be J.J., their father, Emic thought. He was much slower and seemed to limp as he steadied himself on the ground, leaning slightly against the side of the rig. He was making a phone call and looking up at the house.

A couple of hours passed and their life lay around them in mountains of cardboard, each scrawled with its proper destination: KITCHEN, BATHROOM, EMIC'S ROOM, BRODY'S TOYS, LIBRARY, etc. She noticed a lamp flickering on and off in the corner of the living room. When she went to check the wiring, she noticed a small black object attached near the base with a tiny pinhole lens. Was this a *bug* someone planted in their new house? Who would want to spy on them and why? She carefully detached the dime-sized square object using her pocketknife and quickly tucked it into her front jeans pocket as the movers came in with the last of the boxes. The limping one eyed her near the lamp and whispered something to the bulky mover behind him. Something was not right here.

seven

MONDAY MORNING CAME and Emic struggled to rouse herself, pulling her covers up over her head. She could feel her heart race a little, not knowing what to expect from the day. She always felt anxious when meeting new people, like when she joined the robotics team at her old school. She glanced over and saw the foot-tall golden trophy from their last competition on the ledge that spanned the length of her room. She sat up in bed and resolved to face this new challenge. The room was lit bright from the round window. Her bed, just below it, must have been facing due east, she guessed, by the angle that the sun penetrated the room.

"Emily, you have to hurry up, sweetie! You don't want to be late on your very first day of school!"

She really didn't care, but she knew that her father had an interview after he dropped her off, and that was important. She moved more quickly, throwing on her favorite bear animal hat for good measure. "Almost ready," she called down as she started to brush her hair, then realizing that it was already hidden beneath the fluffy white fur of a polar bear.

Then a chime. A text. It had to be Luna.

Good luck today! Luna sent.

Thx need it, Emic sent back and tucked her phone in her worn, military-style messenger bag.

A soft knock came at the door.

"Come in?"

"How do I look?" her father asked. He was wearing his sharpest gray suit and the blue, checked tie she had given him for Christmas. "I think it will be my lucky tie. I have a good feeling about this."

"You'll get it, Papa. And if you don't, there'll be a better one somewhere else. Right?" Emic tried to sound reassuring. She recalled some of the conversations she'd had with him. He would sit with his arm around her, trying to give her confidence with just such a reassuring and knowing tone, such as the time she was going off to her first robotics competition. The memory flashed in her mind. She had been so sure she would fail. "Just have fun! Think about what you would do if you were building that robot for yourself. Don't worry about what anyone else is doing. Just focus on what you're doing. And even if you don't win, you will still have learned something, right?" he had told her with his big honest grin. This was the same grin she gave him now as she patted him on the shoulder. For a moment she believed he was recalling the same memory.

They hugged and he stood up to leave. "You better come down and eat a little breakfast. We really should leave in the next ten minutes."

"Okay. Be right there." Emic tied the laces of her blue wingtip Oxfords. She was wearing a green striped top and bright yellow corduroy pants. She pulled on a fuzzy purple hooded sweater, then stepped in front of her new full-length mirror. She'd never had one before. This one was built right into the wall. She contemplated changing her outfit. She was well aware that nothing she wore matched, and that was intentional. It was a peculiar style she'd developed over years of practice. The more striking the contrast of patterns and colors the better.

Yes, I know. My yellow pants don't quite work with my shirt. And yes, the blue shoes and purple sweater kind of clash, but I think it looks great. Somehow it just all works together. This is me! This is what I like! Deal with it!

This little pep talk lasted only seconds. She gave herself a smirk in the mirror, raised her chin up a few centimeters, still not 100% sure of her decision to go for it and be herself, but she knew in her heart this was what she had to do.

"Be yourself," she said out loud, pointing directly at her image and trying hard to convince herself that the day ahead would go smoothly. Finally, she reached into a box on her dresser, pulled out her grandfather's gleaming medal, and pinned it to her sweatshirt for good luck.

EMIC THOUGHT BACK to those summer afternoons she would beg to go and see Grandpa Gregor at the Shady Grove Nursing Home across town. "Please, please, please? Grandpa really wants to see me and there are so many more stories he has to tell me and he'll be so disappointed if you don't take me and..." By then her parents already knew they would give in. Most of the time they simply dropped her off at the front entrance by the big front porch lined with white rocking chairs. She knew how to sign herself in on the visitors' clipboard at the front desk that was about three inches higher than she was. The staff paid her no attention as she marched up the main hallway to her grandfather's room. When she was eight years old this would happen several times a week. She remembered sitting in the oversized faux-leather chair next to him in his room that he shared with a gentleman who seemed to always be asleep and snoring. One rainy afternoon, a few months before her grandpa died, as they sat and chatted while she drew him little sketches, he pulled out a slim blue velvet-covered case that looked like a jewelry box. It creaked open in his liver-spotted hands and inside was the military medal.

"What's it for?"

"This is called the Distinguished Service Cross. It is the nation's second highest award given for military valor," he said. Emic could see his eyes were wet and he was very solemn. "I want you to have it, my dear. Keep it safe. It means I will always be there to protect you."

"What's valor?" she asked.

"It means I earned it. This is for what I did during the war to help this country. I saved the lives of many soldiers when I was in France. I've kept it in my pocket always to remind me that we fought for this country's freedom and for the freedom of others."

At dinner that evening, Emic had asked her parents what "valor" really meant and her father told her, "It means he showed great courage in the face of danger while he was in battle."

"Wow," she said in awe, giving the gold cross with the blue and red ribbon a little polish with her dinner napkin. After that, the medal became a central part of her wardrobe. She pinned it to dresses, wore it with t-shirts, and sometimes even hung it on a necklace from around her neck. It was more than just an accessory. That medal of Grandpa Gregor's became her most valuable possession. When she was younger it was a source of great pride and often people would remark on it or ask who it was awarded to and for what reason, but as she grew older it seemed to attract silly jokes from silly boys and sideways glances from girls who thought that fashion correctness consisted of shopping exclusively at Justice, Nordstrom, or H&M. These days, she usually kept her medal hidden deep in her pocket. In this unfamiliar place, she didn't need to face a new set of strangers and have to explain its background to them or why she took it with her wherever she went. She just hoped she didn't have to ask anyone for directions to her next class.

The ride to school was a quick five minutes. Just like at her old school, she realized it was probably close enough to walk or bike. On the sidewalks she saw small groups of kids that must have been about her age. Her father was driving her there. Her mother would go on to her new job at the college after dropping Brody off at his preschool class. This was a big day for all of them.

Father parked the car and walked her into the school building. It was a large, gray stone building with forest green shutters. Off to the side, a large sign had "FLAT

ROCK MIDDLE SCHOOL," carved in gold letters on a forest-green background. They climbed the entrance stairs holding hands, something they rarely did anymore, at least not in public, but she was not about to let go of him today. They went to the front office together. The school secretary was sitting behind a sliding window at a desk. She was an older lady with rosy cheeks and a genuine smile. She slid the glass partition open. Her name tag read "Mrs. Cranford" in frilly cursive. She'd obviously made the name tag herself, as it was embellished with colorful flowers and stickers. A matching rosy flower secured with a bobby pin in her curled white hair gave her the appearance of a potential fairy godmother.

"You must be Emily?" she said in a lyrical, deep southern drawl.

"Emic," her father offered. Emic was thankful she didn't have to correct this kind woman.

Mrs. Cranford pulled out a manila file folder and passed it through the window to Emic. "This has your class schedule, teacher list, and a map of the building, sweetie." Next she handed her a temporary student ID card on a lanyard. "You'll have to get your picture taken. Just stop into the media center and have the teacher there take it sometime this week. You'll need this card to charge your lunch and get on the school bus. I see you will be riding the school bus; that will be bus #34. Picks you up opposite side of the street from your home address at about 7:20 AM. Be careful not to lose your ID, dear. This is where your first class is," Mrs. Cranford said in a sweet voice, pointing at the map. "Down this hall, turn left, and then it's on the righthand side. Room 15. Your locker number is 141 and here is your combination." She handed Emic a blue half-sheet and then reached out, giving Emic's hand a warm pat. That first encounter made Emic feel welcome already.

"Thank you." Emic nodded back to Mrs. Cranford, making certain to look her in the eyes.

"Have a good first day. Just be yourself," her father said. Emic knew he would say it, truly predicted it, and yet she was still relieved to hear those words. She knew it was what she needed to hear. *Be yourself.*

Emic walked down the long, fluorescent-lit hallway, filled with boys and girls talking, laughing, checking their lockers on either side of her and going into classrooms. She saw bulletin boards covered with artwork and lists of rules, and posters about being honest and having resilience. A couple of teachers were standing by a doorway talking quietly. When she finally reached Room 15, she heard a loud bang.

"Dublin!" A loud yell echoed into the hallway.

Emic came through the open classroom door just as a stern, thin lady dressed in a gray tailored pantsuit with graying hair pulled back tightly in a bun was peering over and pointing at one of the boys at a desk in the center of the room.

The dark-haired boy was lanky, wore jeans with holes in the knees, and had on an oversized black graphic t-shirt. He leaned over and picked up the book that was on the floor.

"It was an accident," Dublin said, in a slightly sarcastic tone. Emic did not think he looked embarrassed at all.

Ms. Spencer looked over and noticed Emic from the corner of her eye. She coldly directed her to sit down quick with a flick of her hand.

"Emily M. Rizzle?"

"Emic," she answered using the same dry tone.

"Excuse me?" Ms. Spencer responded.

"Emic. I'd like to be called Emic, please."

"As you wish. Please have a seat…Emic. I have some morning announcements to make." Ms. Spencer was obviously still agitated by the falling book incident.

The only empty seat was, unfortunately, next to Dublin, who smirked in what she believed to be a sinister way when she sat down.

So this would be her homeroom and, later in the day, her history class.

Her teacher took attendance using a monotone voice and each student responded with "here" or "present," in a matching manner.

"There will be a bake sale today outside the cafeteria. All money raised will benefit our upcoming field trip to the Biltmore Estates in Asheville. Please remember to have those permission slips signed and returned as soon as possible. Without it, you will *not* be allowed to attend. There will be an assembly tomorrow morning at 8:15 so please try to arrive on time. Spirit Week is next week, so feel free to dress in our school colors: green and gold. Are there any questions? No? You may read quietly until the bell rings." The class fell into silence, apparently the norm for this homeroom.

At her locker, she saw groups and pairings of girls walk by. Most of them had probably been friends for years. Science, history, art, music. Emic kept to herself all morning. Lunch would be a challenge. She made up her mind to sit with some girls she recognized from an earlier class. The cafeteria was huge and loud, but glancing around she spotted them at the far end. She carried her lunch tray over, heads turning as she walked by, and planned to sit down with the three girls. They were in the middle of a conversation and talking over one another. They stopped abruptly when Emic started to put her tray down.

"Hi, um, hello. I'm Emic. We're in art class together."

"We know," the blonde one said, taking a bite of her sandwich and not even bothering to look up.

"Where are you from?" another one asked. The blonde gave her brown-headed friend a quick stabbing look as if to remind her not to speak again to this uninvited intruder.

"Chicago," Emic told them, waiting to see if they had any more questions, then putting her tray down on the table hesitantly, but still standing.

"What *would* you call that mismatched style, anyway?" The blonde emphasized her use of the word *would* with a tinge of disgust and lip curling.

"Corinne, I think that's like, um, called *Harajuku?* I heard about that from my cousin. You know," looking only at the blond for approval to continue, "she's in New York. Anyway, she's got a *crazy*-looking au pair from London and she said it's some kind of Japanese street fashion where they dress like grown up baby dolls and fairy tale creatures and stuff."

"Ah, no, not really, Krissy." They went back to their conversation, acting as if Emic wasn't still standing there. Feeling uncomfortable and unwelcome, after a strained moment she lifted her tray to try another table. Dropping her fork, she stopped and squatted down to pick it up. Before standing, she paused and overheard the girls talking. "It's all *silly*, if you ask me. She *clashes* with us. She can come sit with us when she dresses like a *normal* person." Corinne's loud voice made sure that the other students in surrounding tables around them turned to listen.

"Ouch!" The third girl then giggled. The three of them sat there smirking and proud of their put-down. Still needing somewhere to sit, Emic looked around and saw Dublin sitting by himself in the corner of the cafeteria. Observing her searching, he gave her a wave to come over. It surprised Emic, and she looked behind her to make sure it was she he was waving to.

"Why don't you go sit with punk-rocker boy! The two of you will…*blend*. What? Dublin, did you cut your hair with like a weed-whacker, or something?" the girl continued.

"Oh, tickety-boo, Reegan. Don't be so capricious! You're all just a bunch of toffee-nosed dangleberries."

"What's a dangleberry?" Emic whispered as they turned their backs on the high-pitched snickering trio.

"Fecal remnants adhering to butt hairs," he answered with no pause.

"Oh…kay then. I'm not sure how to respond to that." Emic could not help but laugh at this strange boy. She'd never heard anyone talk like him. "I moved here at the beginning of the year from the Presidio in Monterey," he told her. "It's a military base in California. My dad's in the Air Force—we've moved around a lot. I obviously don't blend in with all the athletes, preps, and brainiacs at this school. In fact, I think they kinda just see me as a technogeek here."

"Why?"

"I got in some trouble for hacking into the school's grading system. I didn't change any grades. A couple of boys just wanted to see if I could do it. They dared me, and I found that it was really quite easy to access."

The bell rang. "Oh no, I left my map in my locker. Can you tell me where to find French class?"

"It's just down the hallway, there, to the right and down the stairs on the left."

THAT WASN'T SO *bad*, she thought, as the last bell of the day rang and she went outside to wait for her father's car to pull up in the car line. Just then, the girls she'd encountered at lunch approached from behind her.

"What's up with that weird bag? Are you going into the army or something?" Corinne sneered.

"Yeah!" she heard from behind her. It was Dublin. "And she's going to have a dicky fit and drive a big tank over your house, ya plank!"

The girls rolled their eyes and walked away, laughing and saying something about Dublin. She learned quickly that Dublin said whatever popped into his head with little thought to what it sounded like. He was quick, and no one could compete with his crazy comebacks.

"Thanks" was all Emic could manage, impressed with his wit and comedic timing.

"Ah, they're just blinkered dimbos. They tend to pick on the new kids, or kids like us."

"Kids like us?" Emic asked.

"We're different, aren't we," answered Dublin in a conspiratorial tone.

"I guess we are." Emic smiled.

EMIC'S FATHER WAS quiet in the car. She knew without asking that he had not gotten the job. Emic reached out and put her hand on his. Breaking the silence, he asked how her first day went.

"It was fine."

"Who was that boy in the black t-shirt with the Union Jack?"

"Oh, that was Dublin. He's in a couple of my classes. He's a *wee* bit different."

eight

THAT EVENING, EMIC's father was busy getting dinner ready, standing over the steaming pot, opening a can of whole tomatoes. Emic was doing her homework at the kitchen table and her mother was, as usual, on her laptop doing something for work. Brody was rolling out Play-Doh pasta and pie crusts.

"Howard. What if you look for something temporary? You like cooking. Why don't you look at restaurants, until something else comes along?" she asked, looking up from her screen.

"Papa, you could be a chef! Didn't you work in a

restaurant a long time ago?"

"It was before you were born, Emic. When I was in college." He smiled at them and said he'd look tomorrow.

After dinner he decided to take a drive. Maybe it was to drive by different restaurants in town to see what was there, maybe it was to get to know the area a little better, or maybe it was just to clear his head. So, with her mother busy working upstairs on her research, referencing the stacks of books around her on her bed and making notes on the computer while Brody played an app on his tablet, Emic thought this would be a good opportunity for her to see exactly what else was in Grandpa Gregor's box. She tiptoed into her father's new study. It was a chaotic assortment of lamps, frames covered in newspaper leaning in stacks against the dark wood paneling, tubes with her father's many architectural drawings, and boxes filled with books and drawing tools. She had to move several boxes to find it, but when she did she saw that it was still sealed. Pulling out her pocketknife, she repeated the process of slyly opening the side of the cardboard box. Soon, she had sprawled its contents all around her on the floor. There was not such a rush this time, so she was able to get down deeper and examine all of its contents.

First, she pulled out a framed picture of Grandpa Gregor standing rigid and in full military uniform. He was standing in front of a shiny car. Flipping it over, she

saw etched on the back in pencil: "1946 Citroen." She'd
seen this car before, in a picture on her father's desk. It had
lots of chrome and smooth edges. She reached in again
and found, wrapped in brown, crinkled paper, a thick pen.
She pulled at its cap instinctively and discovered it had
a razor sharp metal blade where the ink pen tip should
be. Next she found a larger item, fabric covered and tied
several times around in twine. Unwrapping it, she found a
tiny, black camera, almost half the width of her palm. On
its front, engraved in white letters, she read: "No 79958".
From the bottom of the box, she pulled out a black, plastic
pouch. It had a fold in the middle. Inside it were five heavy
coins and three rings all made of real gold! The pouch
seemed to have been taped closed at one point, and it was
difficult to make out exactly what it said on the outside,
but in raised letters she could read:

"IF FOU...ETURN
COM NAV...NAL 34D
NORTH..."

Also in the box were large, old-fashioned envelopes,
the kind that have a small flap on the narrow side with a
hole punched in the center, and which close with bendable
metal tabs. Inside the first envelope were papers that
appeared to be old and fragile. She spread the papers out

and found a small identification card among them. On the lefthand-side of the card was the image of a young face. She could still tell it was her Grandpa Gregor. Below his sepia-toned image were the numbers 6983. The card was about as big as a passport, and the original white had faded to a creamy gray. There was a musty smell to it and it felt fragile in her hands. The card read:

HEADQUARTERS, ARMY AIR BASE
APO 959

THIS IS TO IDENTIFY
COLONEL GREGOR L. RIZZLE
AS AN INTELLIGENCE
REPRESENTATIVE OF THE BASE
INTELLIGENCE OFFICE. HE IS
AUTHORIZED TO ENTER ALL
AREAS, AT ALL TIMES, AND
UNDER ANY CIRCUMSTANCES IN
CONNECTION WITH OFFICIAL
BUSINESS.

(UNRECOGNIZABLE SIGNATURE)
BASE C.O. APO959"

What did all this mean? Emic began to leaf through the stacks of papers that she had arranged as she emptied each envelope. A small, wallet-sized photograph slipped out from one of them and into her lap. It was of a young woman with long dark hair, dark eyes, dark lips. Her lashes were long and her cheeks were high. On the back was scribbled the name *Hélène* in the same flamboyant cursive she had seen on the musty postcards.

The more she inspected her grandfather's belongings, the more questions were raised. Emic's grandfather had been a fighter pilot in World War II. That much she knew. *Why were you awarded the medal? Why did you need a camera and why was it so small? So you could conceal it? From whom? And why did you need to know so many languages and live in so many places?*

Emic was certain she shouldn't remove all of these things—her father would certainly notice their absence when he started unpacking. She decided it would be best to sketch a record of them, take some notes, and look into the matter further when she was at school. She silently retrieved her sketchbook, and was heading back to the study when she heard her father come in through the front door. She froze. Everything was still on the floor! What if he saw what she'd done? He would be so disappointed. So angry! She didn't want to feel sneaky, or let her father think of her that way. Maybe she should tell him, admit what she'd done. Then she could just ask him for the truth.

The heavy sliding door to his study was still ajar. She could see the papers from the angle where she stood in the hallway. She had just come around the corner with her sketchbook when her father saw her.

"Shouldn't you be in bed by now?"

"I was waiting for you," she lied. "I wanted to say goodnight." Emic's heart sank lower, hating the words that fell from her lips. Now she was lying to her father, straight to his face! He could tell something was bothering her.

"Come on. I'll tuck you in. Is everything okay? I know it's going to take some time, starting a new school, making new friends. I'm sure this hasn't been so easy for you. Everything is going to be all right. And don't worry, I'll find some work soon."

Emic glanced over her father's right shoulder and prayed he wouldn't turn around, hoping he didn't need to go into his study.

Thinking fast, she said, "Papa, can you bring me up a glass of water? Can you put ice in it? The filtered water in the fridge door, okay?"

He smiled, must have felt like indulging her for old-time's sake. "After that, go straight to sleep...you have school tomorrow and you'll have bags under your eyes if you don't go to bed soon."

Emic sighed relief, knowing her scheme to distract

him had worked. Howard turned to his left and went to the other end of the house, to the kitchen. Emic sprinted into the study, sliding on stocking feet on the glossy wood floor. She gathered the papers, camera, pen, and coins in chaotic handfuls and tossed them into the box, closed it, pushed it back up against the wall, and placed several other boxes on top of it.

nine

FOUND SOME WEIRD *stuff. belonged to my grandpa. don't know what some of it is!* She waited for a response from Luna, but nothing happened. Maybe Luna had turned her phone off and forgot to turn it back on. *Yin?* she tried again.

She hadn't slept soundly. After her father had tucked her in, she overheard her parents talking about money. "It's important to watch every dime." "You have to take any job you can find." Suddenly, her alarm clock went off. It was an old chicken clock. Slapping at it, Emic missed the button a couple of times before successfully quieting the annoying clucking sound.

At school, she was in a daze. The building itself was much older than her magnet school back in Chicago. There was no pool; there was no robotics team; there were no laptop carts, iPads, or Smartboards in the classrooms. The library was small, and most of the books were worn out from years of shuffling from hand to hand, their spines broken.

"Emic." A deep, soft voice came from behind her open locker door. Pulling the door towards her, she saw Dublin. He was wearing a slightly different black t-shirt, today. He looked at her in an impish way, with a dimple in his chin much like Cary Grant's, she thought.

"What was homework last night?" he asked.

"For history? Read chapter five and write a paragraph about it. You didn't do it?"

"Don't worry. I'm just a bit zonked. I'll just dodge it." Looking down at the floor, Dublin coughed and seemed a bit emotional.

"What's wrong? Did something happen?"

"I gotta go," he said abruptly, turned and walked away.

"I'll see you in homeroom," Emic called after him, but Dublin didn't answer and he didn't turn around. Actually, he was walking in the wrong direction, away from homeroom. *Where is he going?*

At lunchtime, she sat by herself at the corner table.

The three bees from the day before were busy buzzing and glancing in her direction. She pulled out a book and pretended to read and eat. Her stomach was in knots as she tried to ignore the fact that she was alone, trying not to be noticed. As she got up to leave, her shoe caught on the edge of the table. She saw the tray leave the safety of her hands in slow motion. It seemed suspended for a second in midair, before crashing to the floor with a bang that made her feel sick to her stomach. In that instant, the hum and chatter of the cafeteria was reduced to complete silence.

She could feel every pair of eyes on the back of her neck as she knelt over the grand mess. It was spaghetti with meatballs, a carton of milk, and a big oozing dark-chocolate brownie. She could hear a few muted snickers coming from different directions. Then, a moment later, a hand appeared full of paper towels.

"Aren't you Emic? We have science together. My name's Dashandra but my friends call me Dede. Let me help." Her long, dark dreadlocks swung down and almost touched the floor. She wore a funky jumper and tall black boots. Her dark mouth and eyes were wide and friendly against her soft brown skin. Emic immediately recognized the girl. This school was not nearly as diverse as her school back in Chicago, and Dede was one of only four students in the whole school who weren't white.

Dede picked up Emic's book and, without hesitation, began wiping off the red sauce from its cover. They stood up simultaneously. Emic felt like she would have reached out and given Dede a big hug if she'd had a free arm.

"I'm such a klutz!"

"Hey, don't worry about it." And just like that, Emic made a new friend.

IN HISTORY CLASS, she saw Dublin again. Wherever he'd gone, he was able to finish his homework, because he passed it in to Ms. Spencer with everyone else's. He shot a wink in Emic's direction and she sincerely felt relieved for him. Ms. Spencer was wearing a fitted suit similar to the one she wore the day before, but beige this time, and wore the same straight, blank face. *I guess she fixes her hair like that every day,* Emic mused.

Emic used to love history class—the research projects, presentations, and exhibits she'd made in her previous school—but this was different. The class was just a lecture, straight rows of old desks all facing forward, taking notes, regurgitating facts and dates. No partner projects or problem solving. No discussion questions or "what ifs" to reply to. She knew it was going to be a long year if this kept up. She adjusted quickly though, and raised her hand dutifully, craving to ask questions and challenge the teacher, but keeping her passion for the subject hidden. It did not feel welcome. The tests, she was sure, would all be multiple-choice or fill in the blanks.

Finally. Study hall. She approached Dublin with sketchbook in hand.

"Can you help me look something up?"

"Can a monkey find his butt?" he said confidently.

Emic flipped the book open to the pictures of the coins she'd made the previous day. Dublin looked at them, and began scrolling through Google, image after image, page after page on the large, aging Dell monitor.

"Whoa! That's cool! This is an 'Escape and Evasion Gold Coin Barter Kit'! This was used by fighter pilots during World War II if they crash-landed behind enemy lines!" He scrolled down the screen for more information, and then looked up at her, explaining further: "If they were trapped, they'd try to buy their way back to friendly territory with it. Where'd you get this?"

"I have more. Here, look this up." Emic turned to the next page. It was the pen. Her drawing made it look more ominous, like a dagger. She had slightly exaggerated its details.

"Wow! What is that?" Dublin was obviously impressed with it. Emic felt a little embarrassed, realizing how deadly it looked.

"It's some kind of weapon hidden inside of a pen."

Dublin seemed to sense her embarrassment. He

typed. They both sat, staring at the posted images.

"Okay. It's called a Stinger. It says it's an OSS OSE Fountain Pen made into a Stinger."

"What's a Stinger?" she inquired.

"It looks like it was something used by spies in the OSS. That stands for the Office of Strategic Services. This page is all about World War II and espionage." They looked at each other. There was a pause.

"Blimey! I think your grandfather was a narc."

"A narc?"

"A spy! Was he a spy?"

The word hung there and Emic's mouth would not release a sound. She didn't know what to say, what to think. "I don't know."

Snapping up and shutting the sketchbook, she rose to leave. "It's almost time for P.E. See you tomorrow. Thanks."

"Yeah, see you tomorrow." Dublin stayed behind, eyes glued to the screen, distracted by something he was reading now. "Is there more?" he asked without turning in her direction.

"I'll show you tomorrow," she called as she raced out into the hallway to breathe.

Who did Grandpa work for? What secrets had he known?

WHEN EMIC GOT home, her father was sitting at the kitchen table, his head buried in his hands. She guessed he'd gone on another unsuccessful job interview. Another rejection, no doubt.

"Hi, Pumpkin. I didn't hear you come in." He hadn't called her that in years. He looked tired. She knew he was upset and his cheery tone didn't fool her. Emic was not easily fooled—she could see right into her father, knew exactly what he was feeling, what he needed.

"Let's make some biscotti," she urged, fearing that her smile was a little too bright, her voice a little too enthusiastic.

"That's a great idea!" he agreed, rising from the table and running his hands through his shiny, dark hair. They were both intentionally putting on a good show, but the act was actually making them both feel better.

The pair of them spent the next hour together in the kitchen, mixing, chopping, baking, and slicing. When they were fresh out of the oven, they sat down together with their hot mugs of brewed tea, dipping in their warm cranberry pistachio biscotti.

ten

THE CHIME WOKE Emic. It was Luna! The chicken clock glowed 2:35.

Yang! was the first text. It was a reference to her *Yin* text a couple of days earlier.

hi! I was grounded. hit charlie at school. got cell back tonight from gran.

y didnt u txt earlier? asleep here

:0 sorry. fell asleep. home today. mom not doing so well. visited her in hospital. just woke. didnt want u to think I was blowin u off. miss u friend.

miss u too. sorry bout ur mom. call me tomorrow. catch

up time? wait. why hit charlie?

he pinched my bottom!

oh. good reason! gtgb.

night

night

Emic could not fall back to sleep after that. She missed her old school. She missed Luna. She missed being on the Robotics team. The moon was bright through her large round window and the attic room was illuminated by its blue glow. Finally she decided to make something. She rubbed her eyes and pushed off the covers. She threw on an old blue sweatshirt that her father had given her and went into her workroom. The naked light bulb dangled above her, swinging slightly from her pull of the long chain cord.

Flipping through the sketches, she came across the page with the miniature camera, and decided she needed to resume her search for the truth about Grandpa Gregor.

THAT DAY AT study hall, she approached Dublin with the picture of the tiny camera.

"Let's see what else we can find out," Emic whispered, leaning in close over Dublin's shoulder. Dublin bounced his head in agreement. He seemed thrilled to restart his efforts to help her on this quest.

"This is a Russian spy camera! This is worth some

money!"

Emic recalled the conversation her parents had had about not eating out anymore, her mother taking on extra work at her new job grading papers and working longer hours; her father accepting a job as a fry-cook at the local Flat Rock Diner.

"Let's sell it. Can you help me put it on eBay?"

"Sure. I need a digital image of it first. Can you get me a picture of it? Take a few, even, from different angles, okay? Here's my email address." Dublin jotted it down on a scrap piece of paper and handed it to her. "Send them to me as attachments. I already have an eBay account, so we can put it up right away. Are you sure you want to sell it?"

"Yes."

That afternoon, Emic asked her father if she could borrow his digital camera to take some pictures. He thought nothing of it. Howard would be leaving home at 4:30 PM for his new line cook job at the local diner. He would be preparing for the early dinner rush. Her mother was not yet home from teaching a biology class at the local college, and would probably not be back until dinnertime.

"Don't forget to do your homework," he said, as he prepared to leave. "Oh, and how was school today?" He always remembered to check up on how she was doing at her new school.

"Good," Emic answered, and it was.

Her father stood at the door as if not really wanting to go. "Okay, good. Well, I left some food in the refrigerator that your mom can heat up in the microwave later. I won't be home until your bedtime. Brody, be a good boy," he said, patting him on the head like he was a puppy.

"Will you come up and say goodnight when you get home?"

"Sure." Emic knew he enjoyed their nightly routine as much as she did. Brody chimed in: "Night night," and Emic corrected him: "Bye, Daddy." As soon as her father closed the door, Emic led Brody into the kitchen and took the tablet off the charger. Brody followed the tablet with his eyes, imploring "Gimme, gimme." Emic grabbed his quilted floor blanket on the way upstairs and Brody trustingly followed his big sister. Emic spread the quilt on the floor, just inside their father's study.

SHE THEN RETRIEVED her grandfather's old camera and used her father's digital one to take a dozen or so pictures before replacing it in the box. As she was closing the lid, she noticed a slim strap sticking out of one edge, at the bottom. She tugged at it, causing the base of the box to pop open to reveal a brown, leather journal. On the inside cover, she read:

Colonel Gregor M. Rizzle
1941-1943
New York

She flipped through the journal. It was filled with scrawled, unconnected notes, and diagrams of strange contraptions. Many things she could not decipher. On most pages there was the capital letter *T* followed by quotation marks, numbers, arrows, and quickly scribbled pictures. Why was the journal hidden? What did the "T" stand for? Then she came across this passage:

August 12ᵗʰ, 1938

Nikola Tesla is the most brilliant man I've ever known. In his never-dimming mind, he holds the secrets that will release our world from its dependence on fossil fuels and electricity. This "free energy" should be shared with the world! Our government wants to keep his plans secret and utilize them for military purposes. We are quickly approaching war with Germany, and it is only a matter of time now, before our nation has to act. It is unavoidable. My time with Tesla is short so I will capture as much of his knowledge here as I am able. Perhaps someday I can share this free energy with the world.

Who is Nikola Tesla?

His name was vaguely familiar to her. Emic put some marshmallows in a bowl, and Brody dutifully took them and climbed into his chair at the table. Emic then turned on the family's desktop computer, which was set up in a small nook in the kitchen, and typed "Nikola Tesla" into Google. *He invented radio? Remote control? Alternating current? Why haven't I heard about him in school? Why isn't he in all the history books?* Here was a man that everybody should know about, and yet it seemed he was intentionally ignored!

Why?

Emic tucked the journal into her book bag and emailed the digital pictures of the camera to Dublin. Then the phone rang, and Emic saw on the caller ID that it said ROBERT FEDERICO, Luna's grandfather. Luna was calling to catch up, as promised. "Hold on just a minute, Luna. I need to get some entertainment on for Brody." Luna laughed, knowing all too well what it meant to have a little brother to look after.

Luna and Emic chatted for quite a while. It had been a whole month since the big move. Luna, apparently, had received a Valentine's Day card from Charlie.

"I think he likes you," teased Emic.

"Shut up," Luna squealed over the receiver.

Emic heard the front door open, and knew her mom

was home. "Hold on just a sec, Mom's home". Emic smiled
at her mom. "Papa said to tell you dinner was in the fridge,
ready to be nuked. I've got Luna on the phone, do ya mind?"
She looked over at Brody, indicating a silent changing of
the guard. Sheila nodded and said "Good to go."

Emic told Luna about her new friends Dede and
Dublin. She mentioned about a funny incident that
happened in art class. They laughed. Luna told Emic that
the robotics team lost their last competition and that
Mr. Harris's budget got cut so they weren't going to go
to Nationals this year, even though they qualified. Finally,
Emic told her old friend about the items she'd discovered
during the move. She explained how she was going to sell
the camera on eBay and give the money to her parents to
help out.

"Are you sure? How will you explain to them where
you got the money? You can't just say you found it on the
sidewalk on your way to school!"

"Oh, I hadn't thought that one through."

"Does it even work? Does it have any film in it?"

"I don't know."

"Well, don't just open it, make sure it's wound up all
the way. My mom still uses an old film camera—you have
to make sure the film doesn't get exposed to the light when
you open it. She's so old-fashioned."

"How is she doing, Luna?"

"I think she's doing better. That's what the doctor told us. The chemo has been rough. My brother, Sol, you know he's only three. He just doesn't understand what's happening. Em, it's just not fair. Why did she have to get cancer?"

Emic didn't know what to say to her friend. How could she comfort her? How could she possibly understand what Luna was going through? She could not even let herself imagine how horrible it would be if one of her parents got sick. There was nothing that she could do or say to fix this for her best friend.

"You know I'm here for you," she said after a long moment.

"Thanks. Just be there," Luna confirmed.

"Wait a minute. I'll check to see if the camera has film in it." Changing the subject, Emic carried the phone with her into her dad's study, careful not to make noise as she pushed the heavy sliding door back into its slot in the wall.

With Luna on the phone, she spun the dial. She lifted the spool, rewound the film until it clicked, found the button to release the back, and popped it open to find a film cartridge. Her eyebrows raised with the discovery.

"It's got film! I think there are pictures on it."

"Can you get someone to develop them?"

"I don't know. I think there's a photography class in the upper school building. I'll check around and see if somebody can do it. The film looks so old, though, I don't know if they even can."

"Well, how cool would it be to see pictures that your grandfather took during World War II?"

The idea intrigued them. They finished their long-awaited call, promised to text more often, and said,

"BFN Yin."

"BFN Yang."

Emic pocketed the film cartridge and returned to the kitchen to check email and shut the computer down. She saw that there was an email from Dublin:

> To: *emic667@yahoo.com*
> From: *dublinrocks@hotmail.com*
> Subject: *spy camera*
> E,
>
> *It's up on eBay. Now we'll wait and see what happens.*
>
> *See you in homeroom.*
>
> D

DUBLIN WAS WAITING for her, arms crossed, legs crossed, leaning on her locker.

"It's already up to $1,400," he said in a smug voice, "just since I last looked at it this morning before school!

Who knows how much it will be seven days from now when the bidding ends."

"Are you kidding me?" But she knew he wasn't, judging by his growing giddy tone, a side of him she hadn't seen before. He wasn't kidding at all.

"I'm serious. You've really got something special here. But I got some weird private messages about it—questions. They wanted to know if it's authentic and where I got it from and if there is anything else where that came from."

"What did you tell them?"

"What do you think? I told them your grandfather was a spy! That little tidbit makes the item much more valuable," Dublin shared proudly. "And the fact that you're his granddaughter gives the camera its *provenance*. I learned that from watching *Antiques Roadshow*."

"Wait. Did you tell them his name?"

"Sure."

"It had film in it, Dublin," she whispered. "Can we get it developed? What if he really was a spy? What could be in the pictures?" She extended the cartridge out to show proof of its existence.

"We're going to find out!"

Dublin explained that he had an older cousin, Scottie, who could help them. He was a senior and had access to the darkroom on the upper school side of campus.

Dublin reached out his hand for the cartridge, but Emic snapped it back, tucking it in her messenger bag in a small compartment at the back with a zipper.

"I'd like to be there when he develops it," she insisted. Dublin agreed, and they walked together to homeroom.

eleven

EMIC SAT IN her tiny workroom. She knew her father would be home any minute. She slid back the lid of the wooden cigar box. It creaked at the back hinges. She glanced through the small, clear packet of postcards. The postmarks indicated that they were all sent between 1944 and 1946. She inspected every detail with an old magnifying glass she'd acquired at an estate sale she visited with her father. He loved to salvage architectural treasures, like mantelpieces or columns, and reincorporate them into some of his jobs. Emic made a mental note that they hadn't been to one in quite a while now and they used to go practically every weekend together. Inevitably, he would buy her a hot chocolate along the way on colder days, or take her out for an ice cream when the weather warmed. Emic really enjoyed her free days, days when Brody came home with Mom; days when she had an hour or two just by herself at home.

She held the military medal up closer to the light and carefully sketched each letter, each mark, each line, filling in the image appropriately with rich colors to match. Tomorrow, she'd investigate exactly why Grandpa Gregor was awarded this medal. She assumed it was his, as it was amongst all his things, but she felt unsure of almost everything these days.

She pulled the journal out again, planning to read more that night. What was he hiding? Flipping through, Emic saw something labeled "T Generator." Under it was the quote:

> *Electric power is everywhere present in unlimited quantities and can drive the world's machinery without the need of coal, oil, gas, or any other fuels.*

Next to it in cursive, a very distinctive and different handwriting:

Free energy for all the world! This will change everything!

She recognized this to be her grandfather's handwriting.

She heard the sound of heavy footsteps coming up the stairs. She stashed everything back in the box, covering it up with a sweater, and yanked down the cord of her light so intensely that she broke the chain right off. Emic stealthily closed her workroom door and was in bed with the covers under her chin by the time the latch to her door was lifted.

"I heard you moving around. You should have been asleep by now, Em. It's very late."

He smelled of frying grease and some kind of cleaning product that made her nose burn a little. His pants, originally white, were stained with food, now red and black and brown. His hands were red. His cheeks were lit on fire and his hair was a sweaty, dark mess.

"Papa, you need a shower. You stink."

"Oh, do I?" He laughed and leaned in closer to tickle her. She covered her nose, squirmed and giggled. "Yes, well, goodnight now. I'm going to go hose down. Go to sleep, little one."

"I'm not so little anymore," Emic said to remind him.

"I know. I just like to say that. I'd like to still believe

that." He kissed her on the forehead and turned her bedroom light out.

"NINETEEN HUNDRED AND fifty dollars, and still six more days to go! And someone's been emailing me saying they're from the International Spy Museum. He says he's a curator and espionage historian in Washington, DC. I think we should get back to him. He says he wants us to take the camera down off the site immediately, that he would like to make us a special offer. What do you want me to do?"

"I think we need to find out what's on that film!"

"Scottie said he could meet with us after school today. Are you game?"

"Sure, I'll just have to let my dad know I'm staying a little later after school so he doesn't wait for me to get home."

Emic texted her father and he was fine with it. He must have assumed she was working on a school project. He did not ask her what she was doing. He trusted her and she knew she was betraying his trust. She felt that knot in her throat come up, just like when they were moving, when she was saying goodbye to Chicago, to Luna, and to that beech tree with their special tree house built in it. They would never build one here. Their yard in Flat Rock was just that—flat and rocky. There were some scraggly bushes, a bed for a flower garden on the side, but no trees that could hold a tree house, much less a swing or even a hammock.

THEY MET SCOTTIE at four o'clock by the back entrance of the upper school. The two schools were next door to one another and shared several athletic fields and other buildings. The buses had all pulled away, and most of the kids had been picked up, or were walking home.

"With the age of these negatives, I'm not so sure if any images will appear," Scottie warned them. "I've never developed anything except regular film before. Well, here goes!" Scottie stepped to the back of the small room and turned out the lights. The three of them were standing there in pitch black. Emic could hear Scottie pry open the cartridge, roll the strip around a metal reel, and then heard the reel sliding down into a metal canister. Once Scottie had replaced the canister lid, he turned on what he called the "safe light," making the room glow a purplish blue. He worked with efficiency and speed, filling the can up with water from the sink and pouring in another liquid.

"Now I'm adding in the developer and we'll see what happens. Don't get your hopes up—it might be too brittle to work with." He banged the can up against the side of the counter, then set a timer that was leaning against the back of the sink. Every half a minute or so, he picked up the canister, turned it upside down and back several times, and set it back down again. Finally the timer went off. He added more water to the can, added something called "Hypo-clear," and shook the can again. He poured all the liquid down the drain. He washed the film for about ten minutes in "Photo-Flo" mixed with water. He finally unrolled the film off its reel and hung it up on a line above them with a clothespin to let it dry.

His large, black-framed glasses kept sliding down his fairly large nose as he inspected the brown plastic strip. He was at least a foot taller than Emic, but about the same width. She could tell that Dublin and Scottie were related. Emic and Dublin were on opposite sides of the filmstrip as it dangled there before them, squinting to see if any images appeared. There were definite shapes; darks and lights.

"We've got something!" Dublin announced, but it was impossible to tell exactly what was there on the small negatives. People, maybe? And objects of some kind. But of who and what? Each of the twelve rectangular brown plates held secrets, and Emic was anxious to see their secrets, secrets that were at least seventy years old.

"All right, listen, this is going to take a while. It's getting dark. Why don't you two go on home, and I'll stay here a while and develop all the pictures from this. Dublin, I'll call you later and tell you what's on them, and you can let

Emic know. Okay?"

Dublin walked Emic home. By the time they reached her block, the streetlights had all come on in the neighborhood and passing cars had on their glaring headlights. She lifted the cement garden bunny at the bottom of the three steps leading up to her front door and found her spare house key. She had returned to an empty house. The only lights on were the porch light and a lamp in the hallway entrance.

"Well, goodnight. You gonna be okay? Nobody's home."

"Sure. My mom will be home soon. And Dublin, thanks for all your help, you know, with—"

"The spy stuff."

"Yes, that," Emic looked down at her key.

"Okay then, night."

He reached his hand out, lifting her chin with two fingers. Emic was biting her bottom lip.

"Glad to help." And he grinned out of the corner of his mouth. This time she knew it was her own cheeks that were flushing red. He seemed so much taller tonight.

Dublin turned to walk back down the sidewalk. "Hey!" Emic let the word escape before she finished deciding what she was going to say next. She just knew she didn't want him to go yet, and then, "Thanks again."

Dublin stopped awkwardly on the sidewalk. She felt

like an idiot, knowing she'd already thanked him.

"I get it. You appreciate me. I know," he said, cracking a grin. He was shambling up the sidewalk a half a block away now and waving his arm back at her to say good-bye. She could feel the heat in her cheeks and involuntarily put the palm of her hand to her forehead.

Ugh! I can't believe I opened my mouth again.

She realized she didn't know where he lived or if it was even near her neighborhood. Was he just being a gentleman walking her home? She decided it could not have been very far away.

EMIC WAS PLEASED that there would be images, but frustrated that she would have to wait to see them. She went about turning on lights. It was after six o'clock and the winter sun had already set beneath the houses and the horizon. She pulled some leftovers out of the refrigerator and started setting the table for dinner. About the time the microwave went *beep, beep, beep,* she heard her mother's keys in the front door.

Something clumsily banged on the frame of the door as her mother came in. "Emily, we have something for you," Mama called from the hallway.

"What is it?" Emic yelled from the kitchen, putting the food down on the dining room table, which she had set with pretty French fabric placemats, cloth napkins, and a lit scented candle at the center. The room smelled of lavender and roses.

"Come and see!"

Emic scooted around the corner in sock-covered feet, skating on the slick floor through the opening of the kitchen into the entranceway, and almost crashing into their mother. Her arms were full; purse, computer bag, keys, and some kind of beige crate covered with a pale blue towel. Brody was giggling and banging on the top of the crate.

Just then she heard it.

"Meooow!" An unhappy, *let me out of this cage right now* kind of noise.

"A cat?" Emic squealed with anticipation of something adorable and furry. "Really?"

"Yes, *really*. I know you've wanted a pet for a long time. I thought it would be nice for you to know you always have someone here to greet you when you get home. He's a little scared, so you'll have to be patient and let him get used to us. He may not want to be picked up right away, so be careful. I got him from someone at work; said he needed a home."

Emic reached out and gave her mother a giant hug full of gratitude and love, causing her mother to lose hold of her purse.

"Does he have a name?" Emic sputtered out, as she

lifted her mother's purse off the floor for her.

"No, you get to name him."

She already knew what it would be. She'd known for a long time. She'd always wanted a pet with this name and finally she had him. Looking down at him, she saw that his eyes were wide and dark, his pupils completely dilated. He was curled up, uncertain, frozen. His ears were laid back flat against his head.

"Oscar," she said softly. She lifted the latch but he refused to come out.

"Here, put some treats just outside his cage. We'll have to coax him."

Carefully, as if tiptoeing, he eased out, then immediately ducked behind his crate to hide. He was black and white, in a pattern that made him look like he was wearing a tuxedo. He backed up underneath the cabinet and decided to hide out for a while.

"He just needs to get used to this place, Em. Just let him be. He'll come out when he's ready."

twelve

DUBLIN WAS NOT in school the next day. She had expected to see him standing there waiting for her at her locker. She wanted to know what the bid was up to for the camera, and what other messages he had received. She was also starting to worry about whether she had done the right thing. Would her parents be angry over the camera being sold? Did it have any sentimental value for her father? Or would they be pleased by how much money it would bring them? Howard seemed to be working almost every night now, and he was always so tired. Maybe he would be able to cut down on his hours, spend more time with her and Brody.

Emic missed her father cooking at home. More than that, she missed cooking with him, the huge mess he made as he used up every pot and pan in the house, sauce splattered everywhere, cheese grated in a bowl and sprinkled all over the counter and all over the floor. He used to make his own homemade pasta and ravioli from scratch. It was his Italian heritage. He had learned it from his mother, Zelda, who grew up in Sicily. And he was a wonderful teacher, showing her just how to press the pieces together after stuffing the ravioli with a homemade ricotta cheese and fresh basil filling.

"DID YOU HEAR that Dublin's dad got arrested?" It resounded over all the other loud voices and laughter. Emic tried to follow it to its source but she couldn't tell from where the words had traveled. She took a guess and went up the stairs, taking two steps up at a time, finally reaching a pair of boys that were discussing the dramatic incident.

"What did you say? What happened? Is Dublin okay?" Emic asked

"Uh, he's okay, I guess. His dad got drunk, I heard, hit somebody's car with his car. That's what I heard. Did a lot of damage but nobody got hurt," the boy said. "And they took him to jail."

"But where's Dublin? Why didn't he come to school?"

"I don't know, but I heard he and his mom went somewhere. Maybe they left. Staying with family, I think," the boy added.

Emic raced home that day. She checked her email and there was still no reply from her friend. She called him and there was no answer. Finally, she got some news: a call from Scottie to arrange a meeting point so that he could give her the photographs. He must know something; she asked again if Dublin was okay.

"They went up to Asheville to stay with some family. He said he'd call soon. I guess it's been pretty rough over there since his dad came home."

"Came home? From where?"

"Afghanistan. He did two tours and I guess it really messed him up. They've had a lot of problems. He's my uncle. My dad told me that some real bad stuff happened over there, and he came back with something called PTSD—post-traumatic stress disorder—and that's why he's so angry and drinking all the time. He needs to get some help before something really bad happens—I guess that's why they left. Hey, you didn't ask me about the pictures."

"Oh, yeah. What are they of? Can you see anything?"

"I think I should just show you. Where did you say you got this film? There're some pretty strange images; a couple of them didn't turn out but the rest are good—"

"When can I see them?" Emic said. "The seventh grade is going to Biltmore House on Monday".

"Okay, got to go, Emic, how about Tuesday after school then, at the middle school playground?" his voice trailed away as the call ended.

"Day after tomorrow," Emic murmured to herself.

EMIC WAS SO glad when Oscar curled up next to her that evening, while she struggled to focus on her homework. She had a slice of leftover pizza next to her on a paper plate, some stale sparking water that had gone flat. Her head was bent down and she was genuinely worried about Dublin.

Her mother came in and asked: "Emily, baby, what's wrong? I know moving must have been hard on you. Are you making new friends? How are your classes going? I'm sorry, I've been just so busy with this new job, and now your father's working all the time..."

"And Mom, we really need to go grocery shopping." Emic said, to change the subject.

Her mother eyed the soggy, sad-looking slice of plain pizza that had grown cold by Emic's elbow. "I'll go tomorrow. Anything special you want me to make?"

"No, just not leftovers or a can of beans."

Her mother sighed. "Now, how's school going? You

don't tell me much about school anymore," her mother continued.

"It's definitely different. I'm still getting used to everything. I miss being on the robotics team, of course— they don't have anything like that here."

"Can't you start one? You and your friends?" her mother asked.

"I don't know. Actually, that's a really good idea."

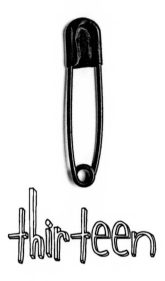

thirteen

ON THAT LONG Friday, Emic felt Dublin's absence in every hallway. When she heard a boy's voice from the other side of her locker door, she quickly shut it, expecting him to be standing there, smirking at her. She was sure the second hand was moving in slow motion as it made its way around the big, white clock face above the exit door to her classroom. Krissy was sitting to Emic's right and had put her head down on the desk at the beginning of class, and now seemed to be drooling on her open biology textbook. Anxious to get home, Emic leaned down to clutch the straps of her backpack five whole seconds before the bell mercifully rang.

"Emic" she heard, just as she reached the archway of escape. She turned to see Krissy with a stupefied look on her face. She held out what looked to be an old postcard: "It fell out of your bag when you bolted." Emic glanced down and noticed she hadn't even zipped up her backpack. Her grandfather's journal had shifted positions and was now visible.

"Hey, thanks." Emic said with a tone of real appreciation.

"Yep," Krissy mumbled and left.

Emic put her bag down on the table and looked at the yellowed postcard. She'd never really looked closely at the postcard before. There was a drawing, labeled "Fig. 6", with what looked like little bolts of lightning and a rotating wheel inside a box. And this message:

Dearest mother and father, I miss you very much.

I finally figured out how to make a rotating magnetic field.

This is how it works. An electric motor can spin by progressive shifting of the Magnetic Field. We could fly a plane with this!

Your loving son, Nikola Tesla

Emic carefully slipped the card back into the journal and hurried out of school. As she walked along the street towards her house, a large black car drove up the street towards her. Inside were three men wearing suits. As the car passed, one of them turned to look at her. She didn't really pay much attention, because moments later, as she reached her house, she saw Oscar in the front yard, crouched down as if he'd seen a mouse. "Oscar. What are you doing outside?" She picked him up, nuzzling him into her. Then she saw how the cat had escaped: the front door was open a crack. Was her mom home early? Maybe she and her dad hadn't closed the door securely when they left?

"Mom?" she called out. No answer. As she plopped her bag and Oscar down, she looked up to see scattered papers at the entry to her father's study, and the door ajar. Frozen for a moment, she called out more hesitantly: "Hello?"

Inside the study, some boxes were turned upside down, and she could tell that many were missing altogether. In a panic, she bounded up the stairs to her room, rushed back to her workroom, flipped open her toolkit and carefully lifted out the top tray to find the black journal still there. She sat back in relief. In that moment, she was certain that whoever broke in was after the Tesla journal. She carefully replaced the journal, and slid the toolkit farther back into the darkest corner of her workroom. She knew she had to talk to Dublin.

She was still shaky and unnerved by the break-in, when a sudden bang from the floor below made her jump. Were they still here? She could hear footsteps coming up the stairs. Emic's breaths were quick and shallow as she quietly pulled the wooden door next to her closed. She heard a knock, then another.

"Sweetie? Emic, are you in there?" her mother had obviously noticed the destruction downstairs. Emic opened the door to a barrage of ever-louder questions. "Are you okay? I called the police. It looks like we've been robbed! Did you see anything? Why are you hiding? Why didn't you call me?"

"Mom," Emic shouted. "Calm down! I just got home. Oscar was outside. I think they took some boxes of Grandpa's, that's all. I didn't see anybody." She lied.

As Emic was getting ready to go to sleep that night, with Oscar curled up at a safe distance at the foot of her bed, her cell phone chimed that a message had been received. *Finally!*

It was a text from Dublin.

Heard the police were at your house what happened!?!

Robbed took some boxes saw three guys think lookin for the camera

wow camera over 2300!

r u ok? heard u went to asheville.

What seemed like a few minutes passed by and there was no sound. She lay there and stared at the blank screen.

dad got into some trouble. Ill be back soon I think, he finally replied.

sorry, Emic sent.

fourteen

It was Saturday at last. Her father worked the lunch crowd at the diner so he could be home for dinner that night. All of them seemed determined to have a good evening and forget about the break-in; they needed to restore their newly found sense of "home."

Emic was thankful not to have to eat take-out, or another one of her mother's "kitchen experiments." Sheila was a great researcher, but not a great cook. Howard liked to tease her and say she could make food for the astronauts but it wouldn't fly with Joe Public. "Sheila, what have you been feeding the poor children? Let's make a big Italian supper tonight. How does that sound?" her father asked as he closed the refrigerator door.

"I'll help, Dad. Let's make something good. Your homemade sauce?"

"Okay, get out the olive oil, the fresh basil, and the can of San Marzano tomatoes. I'll start crushing the garlic and grating the pecorino."

"Howard, don't go too heavy on the garlic. I reek of it for days after you make your homemade sauce."

"Gravy! It's called *gravy*," he said in his best Italian accent, laughing and looking more like his old self. He emptied the tomatoes into the pan with the garlic-infused oil, and they sizzled. "Ba, da, boom! That's red gold," he said, holding up a spoon of sauce. Then he put on some music, which began to filter throughout the house...it was Louis Prima, his raspy baritone voice singing "When You're Smiling."

The feel in the kitchen was festive and everyone was happy to be together. It felt like old times. "Papa, you are so good at cooking, so why do you work at a diner? Why don't you just open up your own Italian restaurant? There's nothing like that here—I think people would love it."

Howard was busy fine-chopping some fresh basil, which he had first rolled up like a cigar on the cutting board, with a large, sharp knife and added it to the pan.

"You make it sound so easy, Em. It takes money, a *lot* of

money, to open up a restaurant. And we just don't have it."

"How much? What do you need to start? Can't you get a loan?"

"Maybe. I would need ten thousand, maybe more."

"Howard, you used to dream about that—owning your own restaurant. Maybe now is the right time. I wonder if there's any way…" Her mother trailed off, not wanting to spoil the mood. The song ended and there was a lull. Then "Jump Jive & Wail" came on, and Howard began to dance around the kitchen. He was an enthusiastic dancer and he reveled in it, seeming to make fun of himself with his big grin, lanky arms, and exaggerated movements. Emic had always been embarrassed by it, but she was so delighted to see him doing it now. Dad grabbed Mom and he danced with her there by the stove, Emic laughing with red cheeks. Mom laughed and pushed Dad away, as he made her sway back and forth to the beats of the rhythm. As the song ended, and her mother returned to setting the table, her father began toying with the idea of what Emic had proposed.

"So let's say I open my own restaurant," he began, playing along. "What would we call it?"

"Celianna's, after Great Aunt Celianna."

"Celianna's Italian Restaurant," he said while turning the knob to boil by the burner to boil the water. "I like it." He diced onions with some butter into a pan to sauté.

He used the spatula with great precision as he effortlessly mixed, sniffed, added salt, tasted. It was as natural for him to be in the kitchen cooking as it was for Emic to be building some contraption. He pulled out an invention that Emic had made for him to help cut and crimp the raviolis. She often made unusual gifts for people for Christmas or birthdays. She put much thought into them, making her creations useful and something that they needed.

"This *is* pretty ingenious. We should get a patent on it. I bet it would really sell!"

"Papa, I'm not sure how many people actually still make their own pasta."

"Good point. But still, you do think up some terrific gadgets."

"And we could use the money to open your restaurant." Emic announced.

Emic's cell phone rang. She saw that it was Dublin.

"I'll be back in a minute, Papa." She walked into the sitting room and sat down on a footstool by the window. "Dublin? How are you? Are you back?"

"Emic, my mom's left my dad, and I'm not sure if we're coming back. I wanted to let you know that I got an email from someone at the Smithsonian Institute; and someone else sent an inquiry about the camera. They want to know if the film winder works and I emailed back that we knew it worked because there had been a roll of film in it. I added that to the description on the bidding page, and all of a sudden a lot of people wanted to know about the film: what was on it; whether or not they could bid on it separately!"

"The Smithsonian? What did they want? Hold on—how do we know that the people that contacted you are actually from the Smithsonian?"

"Exactly. And how do you know if some of them aren't the same ones that burgled your house?" Dublin added.

"So, what do they want?"

"They want to meet with us. They want to see the camera in person, but they also want to know what was on the film."

"I talked to Scottie," Emic told her friend. "He said that he got about ten pictures to come out. He didn't tell me exactly what they were of, except some of them were of a woman. Could it be Hélène—the one that wrote the postcards to my grandfather?"

"Hélène. Hold on. Let me look something up."

There was a silence as Dublin was typing, searching the Internet.

"Could this be her?" Then he began reading. "It looks like there's a book about her. It says:

> Nancy Wake, also known as Hélène, is one of
> the true heroines of World War II. Born in New
> Zealand, she was living in Marseille when the

Germans invaded. Wake became active in the Resistance movement; she smuggled messages and food to underground groups in Southern France and helping refugees flee to Spain. By 1944, Wake was on the Gestapo's most-wanted list. The Germans nicknamed her the 'White Mouse' because she was so difficult to apprehend. After six attempts to capture her, Wake escaped to Britain—where she became a British Special Operations Executive. Wake parachuted back into France and became a leading figure among the resistance. This book tells the extraordinary story of this exceptional woman."

Nancy Wake. Emic remembered seeing something about her in one of the letters, which was signed with the name "Nancy". She thought she might go back into the box that night and get a better look.

Was Nancy the Hélène of the postcards? Why had she written to my grandfather? Did he write her back?

"Hey, *finito!* Em! Come get dinner!" her father called.

"I gotta go, Dublin. Oh, and Dublin, there's a journal! We'll talk tomorrow."

The kitchen was thick with the scents of chopped garlic and fresh basil, and steamy from the draining pasta. It was rare these days to sit together as a family, and it felt like a special occasion, a true celebration.

Emic looked over at Brody, pasta sauce dripping off his chin. Remembering the DVD box set of *Star Wars* films she got from Aunt B., Emic smiled and announced: "I think I'll get Brody cleaned up and watch movies with him."

Howard's neck went back and his chin doubled while Sheila reacted with a look of disbelief. "Volunteering?"

"I guess that means I get clean-up duty!" Howard smiled as he pulled Sheila towards him into an embrace that spoke better than words. Emic could hear her mom softly singing an old Hank Williams song, "Hey good lookin, whatcha got cookin," as she led Brody up the stairs. They passed Oscar on the staircase coming down, as they were going up. This triggered an unanticipated rendition of "O so lah meow" from Brody.

Later that night, Emic searched for information about the British Special Operations Executive (or SOE) and learned that Nancy Wake had parachuted into the South of France at about the same time as her Grandpa Gregor—in April of 1944—and the postcards began a few months later after the mission had ended. *Was that when they met?*

THE NEXT MORNING, her chicken clock began to cluck at five AM. With it still dark outside, she quickly roused herself, threw on her robe and slippers, and inched silently past her parents' bedroom down to the first floor. Once there, she spread out the letters, newspaper articles and photographs and, finding what she was looking for, scanned over the letter from Nancy.

> *Dearest G,*
>
> *I'm sorry it has taken so long for me to respond. If only things had been different, perhaps we could have been together. You saved my life that day, and I will always be grateful. Please do not speak of me but treasure what moments we had. I received your half, and now mine is enclosed. You will always be my other half. Our pieces make a perfect fit.*
>
> *Yours Forever in Times of War,*
> *Nancy*

Within the envelope there was half of a crinkly, puzzle-cut dollar bill.

Where's the other half? Why would they send each other half of a cut-up dollar bill?

THE STUDY LIGHT flipped on. At the door stood her father, hand motionless on the light switch, gazing down at his daughter and the scattered contents of the box. Puzzled, he took another step towards her, turning his other hand up as if about to ask a question but his mouth would not form the words. There, on his ever gentle face, was that dreaded look of disappointment.

"What are you doing, Em? It's five o'clock in the morning! Why are you in here?"

She couldn't think of an excuse. Her head slumped.

"Tell me what you're doing looking through Pop's things."

"I found his box when we were moving and I was curious, and then, um, I couldn't stop. I just wanted to learn more about him, I guess. You never really told me what he did during the war, and why he was so angry with the military, and I think he was some kind of a spy, Papa!" she blurted out without pausing for a breath.

Her father stood there, waiting before speaking again, as if trying to think what to say next and perhaps not wanting to say too much: "Why do you think that?"

"Well, the stinger, the coins, the Russian-made spy camera and film."

"You've done some research, I see. Wait. What film? The camera had film in it?" He jerked forward to look inside the box. "Where *is* the camera? Emily what have you done? Emily Michael Rizzle? What did you do with the camera?" he asked slowly, each word coming out accented, punctuated for emphasis. She could tell at that moment that he knew more than he had told her.

Hesitating, feeling as though she were going to be sick, she began telling him her plans for selling the camera, that she knew they were struggling, thinking the money would help. "Now the camera is up to four thousand six hundred and fifty dollars, and ninety-nine cents!"

Her father's eyes widened. "And the film? Is it still in the camera?"

"No, Dublin's cousin Scottie developed it for us. I haven't seen the pictures yet. He's going to get them to me the day after tomorrow, after school. There's more: someone who says they work for the Smithsonian contacted Dublin and wants to meet with us. They're insisting we take the camera down off the site. Why would they do that? What's going on?" Emic felt scared now, realizing that this was a more serious situation. Maybe they could really get into trouble.

He put his arm around her and tried to calm her, seeing her fear and confusion. "Do you know what's on the film?"

"No, there are only about ten images that came out, though, Scottie said."

"I'll come and pick you up Tuesday after school. I'll take the evening off. We need to get back to these people that are contacting you and find out why they're so interested in my dad's camera. Do *they* know about the film?"

"Yes, I think so. That's when the bidding started going up so high, and people started sending us so many messages. Dublin posted that he knew it still worked because there had been a roll of film in it."

"When does the bidding end?"

"In two more days," Emic told him.

"All right then. We have two more days to track down these people and talk to them."

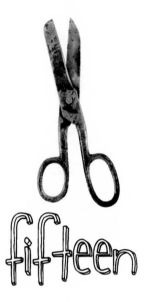

fifteen

EMIC PULLED THE covers up over her head and let out a moan. The idea of riding on a school bus to take a tour of some old southern estate was not her idea of fun.

"My stomach hurts, I think I'm getting sick. Feel my head."

"Come on, sleepy girl, big day today. Up and at 'em. Your alarm clock went off half an hour ago. We still have to pack your lunch. You don't want to be late for your big field trip, do you?"

Her mother sat on the edge of the bed next to her, placing her palm on Emic's forehead, grinning. "You're *fine.* I'll pour you some cereal. Get something to eat and you'll feel better."

"Do I have to go? I won't be missing any schoolwork. I'm old enough to stay home alone, aren't I?"

"Em, let's go." Her mother unsympathetically flung the comforter off the bed, and the sudden chill made goose bumps come up all over her legs and arms.

"Mom." Emic followed this with a growl.

"Ruf," her mother barked from the door before laughing.

Emic had already decided what to wear, so getting dressed didn't take long. She had made her own version of an Elizabethan Tudor hat, turquoise-colored silk fabric, headband finished with sequins. A long sleeved white blouse, the kind with puffy sleeves. It hung nearly to her knees. And, to change things up a bit—she slipped into her one and only pair of yoga pants. At least she would be comfortable.

EMIC SLID INTO a seat that was empty, and stared out the window of the bus that would be taking Flat Rock Middle School seventh graders to Biltmore House. She didn't expect to see Dublin. She quickly scanned the rows for Dede, with no luck.

Did she get put on the other bus? That's just great! Emic thought, sinking down into the sticky brown vinyl seat, and causing that embarrassing friction sound that could easily be mistaken for a bodily function.

Corinne, Krissy and Reegan huddled at the back, giggling and whispering. Sometimes she could catch a "can you believe it?" news flash from Krissy, or a high-pitched "Oh, my God" from Reegan. Then Emic caught eyes with Corinne, who blurted out, "Yeah, she's so weird."

Like fresh air through the bus window into the stuffy, hormone sweet enclosure, Dede suddenly plopped into the seat next to Emic, who let out a noticeable sigh of relief.

"What are the haters up to now? I can tell you're happy to see me!"

"You have no idea just how happy. Up to their usual, backstabbing, gossip… So, have you ever been to this Biltmore Estate?"

"Yeah, I actually go every Christmas with my grandmother; it's a tradition. She just *loves* all the decorations and the giant Christmas tree—we've gone every year since I was three. So, lucky me, this is my second visit this school year. It's pretty cool though, when all the lights are up, and the gift shop rocks! Did you bring any spending money?"

"Uh, no. That would be called disposable income; something my family is a little short on right now," Emic admitted.

"Don't worry, sis, I'll get you something."

"You don't have to do that, Dede, just having you in the seat next to me is gift enough."

The friends hugged and laughed as the bus made its way through the mountain highway to America's largest home. On arrival, after check-in and head count, each student group was joined by a uniformed tour guide.

Emic's group's tour guide began his rehearsed spiel loudly, and with great gusto, overly articulating and gesturing excessively with his hands. He'd obviously either practiced a lot, memorizing his speech like a true thespian; or he'd said the same words so many times that he probably babbled them in his sleep. His dark blue uniform seemed fresh off the rack, with its crisp ironed seams; his freshly polished gold nameplate read: *David*.

"George Vanderbilt, son of William Henry Vanderbilt, decided that he wanted to build a *little mountain escape* in the country; and so in 1889, construction began on the palatial estate. Once made up of 125,000 acres, this now 8,000-acre sprawl is a bit more than a simple cottage in the woods. 85,000 of the original acres were sold long ago to the federal government and were turned into national preserved land. Construction on this house took six *years* to complete, and George finally opened Biltmore's doors to his friends and family in 1895."

Ear piercing giggles erupted from the back of the school group. Emic glanced back just in time to see Corinne winking and waving at the unprepared David. He coughed and recomposed himself to continue on with his monologue.

"With two hundred and fifty rooms, thirty-four bedrooms, forty-three bathrooms, and sixty-five fireplaces, it's hard not to be overwhelmed by the sheer size of Biltmore. Now, follow me as we begin our tour. Please stay with our group at all times; certain areas are prohibited, and are roped off with signage; this way, this way."

As they condensed themselves into rows, inching their way through a monumental hallway, a hand squeezed Emic's shoulder. She almost screamed until she realized it was Dublin!

"Sorry, I got stuck on the last bus—got to school a little on the late side. They were just closing the doors when I hopped on... Ahh, were you worried about little ol' me?"

Emic could feel her cheeks begin to burn. She was thrilled to see he'd returned to school after all, but didn't know whether to hug him, or hit him for not letting her know sooner.

The crowd inched its way through parlors, an atrium, and then arrived at a colossal two-story library. Towards the back of the group, Emic noticed out of the corner of her eye three men in dark suits, huddled together and staring at her. They were the same three that she'd seen driving away from her house on the day it was broken into!

"Hey, didn't we see those guys hanging around school the other day?" Dede was as suspicious as Emic.

"I think they're after me." Emic instinctively hunched down as if to confirm that they must be following her.

David continued with his history lesson: "The two-tiered, walnut-paneled library at Biltmore House contains some ten thousand volumes, and a fireplace surrounded by a carved black-marble mantel. On the second floor of the library, there is a secret door that George Vanderbilt used himself, to come down directly from his bedroom to locate or to return a book." Their guide pointed to the exact spot of its location.

Dublin realized Emic's plan as it was forming in her brain. He nodded to her, and began a diversionary tactic. He tangled himself up in the plush red velvet-covered ropes constricting their pathway, bringing the metal stands crashing hard to the floor with an echoing boom. In the confusion that followed, Emic slipped up the spiraling staircase to where David had pointed out the secret passageway.

"Call an ambulance! He's having a seizure," Dede yelled, as Dublin made his body shake all over, attracting the full attention of the crowd.

"Oh, dear. Oh, dear." One of the parent chaperones became hysterical and fainted into David's arms. Just then, the docent glanced up to see Emic as she slipped into the secret passageway; simultaneously, the black-suited goons realized that they needed to scan the crowd for their misplaced prey.

One called out, "Yo, tour guide! I think you're missing a student."

David glanced down, raising a suspicious eyebrow at the seizing Dublin, who motioned with his hand cutting across his throat to indicate that Emic was in danger.

"I am a *docent*," David said, helping the woozy lady to her feet. "I am an educator trained to further the public's understanding of the cultural and historical collections of this institution."

"Okay, *docent*, you've lost one of your pupils," the big one growled.

David pulled out a walkie-talkie, holding it with precision: "A chicken has flown the coop. I repeat. A chicken has flown the coop. Over."

"We've got to help her. These are bad dudes and they're after her," Dublin whispered to David who was helping him to his feet.

"It's all right, everyone. Let's all just move into the banquet hall. I have no doubt you will be impressed with this room," he continued, as if nothing had happened. "This room is seventy-two feet long, forty-two feet wide, and its walls are seventy feet tall. This hall features a triple fireplace and an enormous organ loft." The three black-suited men quickly slipped away to continue their hunt. Their mission was to detain Emic, and now she was separated from her classmates and alone.

The sounds of voices and footsteps faded away as Emic emerged into the bedroom of George Vanderbilt. She could hear the grunting banter of her pursuers shuffling closer to the secret doorway. Bolting through the other side of the room, Emic wound her way through a maze of tourists, bedrooms, bathrooms, and down a narrow set of back stairs. She ventured into a basement containing a swimming pool, gymnasium and changing rooms, reaching at last a bowling alley.

When she arrived there, she heard a loud "brawkk-AWK!" as another docent squawked into his walkie-talkie.

Within seconds, David's voice came from behind her. "Can I show you the sub-basement?" Emic didn't hesitate, as they slipped past the crowds and back through the big Banquet Hall. "I hear you're in trouble," he whispered, then, continuing in his docent voice, "That dining table can accommodate sixty-four guests." He pointed over his shoulder, before moving a set of velvet ropes aside for her to pass. They escaped through a door that led downstairs. Instantly, he turned into a disciplinarian barking orders: "Don't step on that rug; don't sit on—or even touch— those chairs. Please keep in mind that this is not an area for visitors."

David pointed to a former coal bunker, closed off with chain-link fencing and filled with cast-iron machinery parts stuffed haphazardly into cardboard boxes. "Every house has a junk room," he snickered. "This is my favorite place in the house—more so than all those lavish bedrooms."

They passed a row of coal furnaces, and he pointed to their O-shaped mouths, exclaiming, "I've been in there!"

"Why are you helping me?" Emic asked, as they entered the servants' quarters and made their way to one of the main kitchens.

"I'm a man in uniform and you seem to be a damsel in distress." He winked at her. "Plus, I was getting bored. What do they want from you, anyway?"

"The secrets to Free Energy. I have Nikola Tesla's missing journal and the government wants it back, but I have no intention of letting them get their hands on it."

"Well, then. Follow me."

Just as they were coming up a small stairway, the walkie-talkie spat out, "The foxes have entered the chicken coop. The foxes have entered the coop." The three goons appeared from around the corner. "I think we were just called foxes," one of them sneered. "What do you think of that?" The biggest of them grabbed David's arm and put an enormous hand over his mouth. Another one snatched the walkie-talkie away from him before he could make a distress call, and hurled it down the stone stairs, causing pieces of it to pop off in all directions and bounce noisily around the enclosed space.

"I don't think you'll be calling anyone on that now," the suit-in-charge said in the same way every bully spoke.

"Run," David yelled, as he slithered out of the handgrip and dashed back up the narrow staircase. Emic dodged back into the maze of rooms, ending up in a working kitchen. Women in white aprons with powdered hands and hairnets were busy preparing food for an event of some kind. They didn't look up from their preparations in time to notice her, as she dodged past them and into a pantry cupboard at the back of the room. From inside, she could hear the trio of men charging into the room and flipping open doors and cabinets, then a large metal pot banging down to the stone floor and a gruff woman's voice yelling, "Get out of my kitchen!"

"This area is restricted. You cannot be in here!" She hit an intercom button on the wall. "Security! Security! Unauthorized visitors in the kitchen."

"Okay, we're leaving, but if you see a girl with dark hair, call this number. *Immediately*. Here's my card. We're from the Office of Alien Property and she has something that belongs to us."

"The office of what?" she snorted, as she tucked the card into her apron and pointed them back to the exit.

Meanwhile, Dublin and Dede strategized while the rest of their group crowded inside a gift shop, lifting little glass snow-globes, flipping through colorful Victorian calendars or playing with small trinkets and dolls.

"Where's Emic? We've got to find her. We can't let them get to her."

They saw David, looking rather flustered, and gathering all the docents together: "Docents, contact every security guard: let them know we have trespassers on the estate. You two, follow me. I have a plan!"

Still crouched inside the small pantry cupboard, Emic overheard David's voice over the intercom speaker: "Attention, ladies and gentlemen; if the lady who was interested in the coal furnaces wants an answer to her questions, she should come to the front entrance." The kitchen staff were a bit surprised by Emic's unexpected emergence from the cupboard, but went right back to their duties.

As Emic made her way to the destination and caught sight of David, she noticed two security guards pointing the three men in the wrong direction, apparently following signs out to the stables. Emic, heartily shaking David's hand in appreciation, made her way out of the front entrance to join up with her relieved friends and mount the steps of the school bus—and her chaperones never even noticed that she'd been missing.

sixteen

"HEY, WHAT'S UP?" Emic whispered, leaning over to Dublin who had pulled his sweatshirt hood up over his head, letting it hang down in front of his face. He seemed strangely sullen. Dublin did not respond to Emic—he was a turtle hiding in his shell and seemed to have no plans of coming out.

After homeroom, he managed to escape more quickly than she, but Emic was resolute in finding out what was going on. She needed an update on the auction; plus she wanted to tell him that she would be getting the pictures that afternoon from Scottie. Wasn't he curious, too?

Finally stepping in front of him as they were in between classes, and putting her hands on her hips to indicate her impatience with this cat and mouse game, she blocked his pathway into the boy's bathroom. She had cut off his escape route and he knew he was defeated.

He sighed. "It's my dad—he's still in jail. My mom says she's going to divorce him, says she can't take it anymore. I don't know what's going to happen; I'm not sure where we're going to live. I think she's looking at apartments, and as if things just couldn't get any worse, my laptop is dead and we can't afford a new one, so now I'm off the grid. There. I just don't want to talk about it anymore." He tried to dodge around her.

"So we won't talk about it anymore. I get it! Scottie's meeting me with the pictures after school today. Do you want to see them?"

"He already told me—most of them are of some woman. And there are a few pictures of some strange machine floating in the background—a flying machine— and your grandfather standing in front of it with two men in long white coats. Oh, by the way, someone called my house about the camera, said they were sending some associates out here to talk to us—they said they wanted to see everything we had that belonged to your grandfather."

"Do you think it could be those same guys from yesterday?"

"Dunno, but they also sent contact details and a request for more information through my eBay account. Oh yeah, and to look for the Research & Development laboratory message from a Dr. Steven Greer. I don't know what that's about."

"The flying machine. There were a lot of sketches of it in my grandfather's journal. That must be what Tesla told him about—how to make it work. And then when my grandfather went to France, he found some guys to help him actually build it! Wait! You told them about my grandfather? What else did you tell them?"

"I just said you found the old stuff in a box, that's all. And then they said they needed to meet with us, and I said whatever, and then they just hung up. What journal?"

"There was a journal hidden in the bottom of the box in a secret compartment. It's filled with all kinds of strange drawings and math formulas."

"Where is it now?"

She patted her messenger bag.

"Whew, I think you should keep that safe." he said, beginning to understand the importance of what she had. "I remember my dad telling me about somebody named Tesla once, when I was younger. Wasn't he a genius inventor or something, but crazy, too? Apparently he had to walk around buildings three times before he could go into them. He once tried to invent something for the military, called a death ray—I thought my dad was just making it all up. Maybe the government guys know that your grandfather knew Tesla. Maybe that's what they're really after—Tesla's secrets!" Just as Dublin said this, two gentlemen in dark suits appeared at the end of the hallway.

"Are you kidding me?" Emic glanced at Dublin as if he had somehow jinxed them by mentioning them out loud. Mr. Dreerden, the principal, was pointing in their direction as the tall men started briskly walking towards them. Emic turned to see Dublin disappearing down the hallway. Emic firmly planted her feet on the floor and decided to face this confrontation, even though every muscle in her body wanted her to run. Just then, Dede appeared, locked elbows with her, and spun her around. "Aren't you coming to assembly? We'll be late— come on." They ducked through the crowd and into the giant gymnasium. Finding their seats midway up on the bleachers, Emic crouched down low, tucking her head down behind a large upper-school boy and hoping the men would lose them in the crowd of noise and sweatshirts.

An unexpectedly loud bang echoed throughout the gym! One of the men had scurried in after her, dodging around the moving mass of students, and had somehow fallen over onto the cart of metal folding chairs. The impact caused an immediate domino effect of banging, one chair against the next. They tumbled forward, until the last one smashed into the janitor who was unstacking them at the other end, earplugs still in ears, and sent him and his mop bucket spinning out onto the gym floor, where he landed in a flying Superman pose at the feet of Mr. Dreerden, who had just stepped up to the podium to take charge of assembly. At this point, one of the suited men charged over and rudely snatched the microphone out of the principal's hand.

"Ms. Rizzle? Emily Michael Rizzle?" His question boomed out at the audience, many of whom were still casually milling around, searching for a place to sit, chatting with friends, or just laughing at the janitor who was slipping about on the spilled contents of his cleaning liquids. Now they started turning, row after row, towards Emic, who tried to ignore the blood rushing up to her cheeks, her face burning with embarrassment:

"Yes? I am Emic," she said, as she stood up tall.

"Will you come with us? We have a few questions we'd like to ask you."

Dede took Emic's arm, and as Emic made eye contact, she asked, "Do you want me to come with ya?" Emic shook her head from side to side, and started to make her way down between the bleachers. When she stepped off the last step and onto the gym floor, she took courage and spoke to the suited man closest to her: "Is this about the item we listed on eBay?"

"Yes, it is. Please follow us." They spoke in a low voice, probably because they did not want to make a scene. It was a bit late for that. As they stood on each side of her, she half expected them to pull out handcuffs, but instead they led her out of the gym and into the lobby of the school, passing Mrs. Cranford's desk. Mrs. Cranford watched with an expression of concern on her face, and Mr. Dreerden followed closely behind.

"What's going on here?" he asked. "I need to see some identification." The oldest of the men took Mr. Dreerden aside, showing him a badge of some kind, leaning in to him and speaking quietly. After hesitating for a moment, the principal waved them all into the conference room next to his office and closed the door quietly behind them.

"This is official government business," the younger one said. The one obviously in charge approached and hovered over Emic: "I'm Special Agent Thomas Connery from the Office of Historical Artifacts. We must insist that you take down the camera from eBay, or we will have it taken down for you, do you understand?" A moment later, another suit, a much larger one, ushered Dublin into the room. He produced a small government-issued laptop from a case, and placed it into Dublin's hands, just as he was sitting down at the conference table. The older one of them repeated the command: "Take the camera down off the site now, before the auction ends." He was firmer this time. His left temple was throbbing.

Is he grinding his teeth? Is he trying to intimidate us?

Dublin looked up at Emic, waiting for her to give the go-ahead. She bit her lower lip, looked down at her hands, and then nodded. Dublin followed their instructions and reluctantly hit the enter key, as the men loomed, standing in a semi-circle behind them.

"How much was it up to?" Emic questioned him at last.

He gulped. "Over six thousand," he told her, shaking his head with closed eyes.

"Wow," whispered Emic, feeling the seed money of her father's dreams for a restaurant slip away.

Special Agent Thomas Connery then took out a cashier's check from his breast suit pocket. "This is a government check for ten thousand dollars, which should more than cover the camera's value. Now, where is the camera and the film that was in it? Dublin's jaw dropped as he stared at the check. Stepping forward, Emic's eyes sharpened: "Why do you want the pictures? What's so special about them?"

She expected some line from spy movies, mentioning "national security." But Agent Connery, with his salt-and-pepper hair and deep wrinkles around his eyes, spoke to them in a gentle manner. "It would be better for you if you did not know too much." The other agents rambled on about "confidentiality" and "top-level clearances," and she didn't understand everything they said. All Emic knew was that Grandpa Gregor had been up to something of great secrecy and the government did not want to let it get out. And then she realized, with a shock, that they had said nothing about Tesla's journal. She suddenly began to feel more hopeful; if they didn't know… perhaps, just perhaps, the journal was still her secret. She decided she would do everything she could to keep the Tesla journal, and her grandfather's journal, out of their hands.

Feeling a new sense of power welling up inside her, she proclaimed: "If you want those pictures, you gotta give me the truth." Her voice was calm and low, head tilted up, eyes straight ahead and set square upon the agent. Had this been an old Western movie, they would now have their hands on their gun holsters, their trigger fingers poised and ready. She replayed the soundtrack of appropriate music in her head:

Who's going to draw first?

The showdown was not quite over, though. The bell rang, breaking their silence and their stare as the halls filled with children and noise, rolling backpacks squeaking on polished floors.

"All right, I can tell you something, but the information I'm going to share with you does not leave this room, do you understand? It is a matter of—"

"National security," Emic and Dublin said it together, in unison with the man. The two larger men glanced at one another with all due seriousness. "All right," Emic said. "I have to call my father now, so he can bring the camera. He'll be here to pick me up at four o'clock."

SCOTTIE MET EMIC, as he said he would, by the Middle School playground at four o'clock sharp. What he had not expected, was the entourage that accompanied her. Dublin stood close by, and waiting behind them were the three men in suits.

"It's okay, they're with me," she said coolly, the words she had rehearsed on her way over from the school building.

"Are these all the pictures?" asked one of the suited men.

"Yes, just ten of the negatives had images on them."

"And the negatives? Where are they?"

Scottie pulled another, thinner white envelope out of his book bag and handed it over to the men along with the larger envelope of black and white photographs, first making sure that it was okayed by Emic. As they left, they were reminded not to speak of this to anyone.

"Don't worry, I made duplicates," Scottie whispered to Emic, as he turned to go. A smirk flashed across her face, as she shared the information with Dublin.

"And the journal?" Dublin asked.

"Safe, too."

EMIC APPROACHED THE driver's side of her father's car. He rolled down the window. She asked, "Got it?" He handed Emic the camera, and she passed it to one of the men who had followed her to the car. Still in a daze, she walked around to the passenger side and got in, plopping down in the front seat. She knew more than her father now, about Grandpa Gregor. She knew things she shouldn't know. She also knew that she couldn't tell him. She was charged with keeping this secret "for the sake of national security."

"So? Did you get the pictures?"

"Uh, no. I guess they didn't come out—the film was just too old, at least that's what Scottie told me." It was a plausible explanation.

"That's too bad. I was curious about what might be on them." They rode along for a time without speaking. "And what's the camera up to, now?" She realized he wasn't angry anymore, and was warming to the idea of selling it off, but the idea of lying anymore made her stomach hurt. It would weigh down on her like a rock for the rest of the evening—she couldn't bear the idea of it. They'd always talked and she'd always shared everything with him.

"Uh, I don't know. I'll have to check with Dublin—the auction ends tomorrow. Papa, if we get a lot of money, will you think about opening Celianna's Italian Restaurant?"

"Maybe. Maybe, Em. Since we talked about it, I've been thinking about your idea quite a bit. I even found a place in town that's up for rent; it was a restaurant once, but has sat empty for the last couple of years; it would be the perfect location."

seventeen

THE PHONE RANG in the middle of dinner. Her father was home, as he had promised he would be, and they were sitting together as a family.

"Let the machine pick it up, honey," her mother said, as she was dishing out second helpings of turkey meatloaf with some gooey brown gravy and lumpy mashed potatoes. It was Sheila's turn to cook, and this was one of about three meals she had mastered over the years. The other two were tacos and mac 'n' cheese (the kind out of a box). "It's been a while since we've eaten together as a family, hasn't it? So, Emily, how was your day? How is school going?"

That was a loaded question and one that she had a difficult time answering truthfully. She voted for the standard line that most of her peers used these days, lacking all detail, all thought, all effort.

"Fine." What else *could* she say? That men working for some unknown branch of the United States government came to school, interrogated her and a friend, and informed her that her grandfather was, in fact, a double-agent spying for both the United States and Russia, sharing secrets about the work of Nikola Tesla in an attempt to bring his inventions to the world, so that future generations would be released from dependence on fossil fuels and have access to free energy?

"Are you working on any interesting projects in your classes?" Howard asked.

"Well, I'm having fun in science class," and that was the truth.

Emic helped clear the dinner table, as her mother began washing the dishes and her father began drying them. She felt lucky in that moment, lucky that they had one another and loved one another so much. The insanity of the day fell away as they planned their evening together:

"How about we put on an old movie." He lifted up a DVD. "*Charade?*" her father asked.

Emic cheered. "I love Audrey Hepburn! Let's make a

big ol' bowl of popcorn with melted butter." This would be the first family movie night they'd had since moving into their new house.

As Emic was popping the popcorn and her father was getting the DVD player set up, her mother called from the other room:

"Emily, honey," she said. "There's a message for you on the machine."

Emic quickly helped clear the dinner table and went to listen to the recorded message. She hit the play button with angst running through her whole being. *Did the government officials call her home phone? Did she get into some kind of trouble over everything that had happened?"*

"Beeeep. Message One, March 16, 7:25 PM," said the machine. Emic helped clear the dinner table, then called back and listened to the recorded message: "Hi Em, call me. It's Luna."

Relieved, Emic dialled her friend immediately.

"I made a new friend," Luna sang.

"Oh? That's good," Emic said.

"Do you remember Charlotte?"

"Sure. Wasn't she the sarcastic one? Her? Really?"

"Really. She's actually quite smart. She's not you, though. You'll always be my Yang. How about you? Has it been tough starting over at a new school?"

"I've made a couple of really good friends—Dede and

Dublin. They've got my back, Yin."

In this moment Emic began telling Luna everything that had happened. She now knew what she had to do. This was too important to keep just to herself. What her grandfather had always wanted was to share Tesla's last and greatest inventions with the world! This journal was the culmination of all his life's work: all of his experiments, all of his knowledge, all of his genius led to the conclusions it contained. This was why her grandfather had entrusted her with the journal! No one would have expected that his granddaughter had the journal in her possession. It's also why he told her all those stories. This would prove, once and for all, that her grandpa wasn't crazy, and that Nikola Tesla was the greatest inventor the world had ever seen!

WEDNESDAY MORNING, EMIC slipped down the hallway at Flat Rock Middle School, but instead of heading to her homeroom, she turned left into the computer lab. At this time of the morning there were no classes yet, so it was empty. She passed by the rows of computers and found the scanner at the back of the lab. Working quickly, she flipped open the weathered leather cover of the journal, and pressed the aging papers down on the glass. Pages were slipping out of the sides, as they had lost their hold on the binding and had come loose. She flipped through to each of the diagrams, drawings, and rambling notes scribbled with barely decipherable text.

Once every page had been scanned in, Emic glanced at the large wall-mounted clock. Seeing that the bell was about to ring for her first class, she finished saving the file to the flash-drive, which was attached to her ID lanyard. Then she tucked the large journal back into her backpack, shut down the scanner, and darted out of the room.

Just as she entered the hallway, students were released from class and were flooding the corridor around her. She made her way to Mrs. Cranford's desk for a late slip and was about to head off to science, when she heard Dublin's voice behind her:

"Heah, Emic, what's up?"

"I'm going to share it all," she leaned into him and whispered. "I'm going to let the world have everything! What can *they* do then? The journal won't matter anymore because the information will be in the hands of everybody!"

"Wait a minute. After all this, you're just going to give it away? You'll be left with bugger all."

"It was never mine, Dublin," Emic said. "It was saved by my grandfather so that it would not get lost, end up as a classified top secret, and only be used by the military. He sacrificed his career and risked his life when he tried to tell people about it, and they made him out to the world to be crazy."

"How did he keep it from them all this time? Why didn't they just come after him?"

"I guess they did and they never found it."

"Well, I'm just gobsmacked. You're off your trolley." Dublin smirked at Emic to see if there was a reaction.

Laughing, Emic shouted, "Oh, shove off."

"Very good. Now, okay then. How are we going to do this, my *wee* one?"

"I think we should meet somewhere neutral, somewhere with lots of people around, in case we're followed again."

"How about Wired, the café down the street from my house and they have free Wi-Fi. Come with me now. I'll get Scottie to give you a ride home."

That afternoon they huddled together over Dublin's laptop with a couple of root beers. They put in the flash-drive, opened the file, and images began to flash across the screen.

"Well, that's a stunner." Dublin smirked again at Emic, who punched his arm this time for saying yet another expression in British slang, nudging him to get down to business.

As he clicked away, the images uploaded in seconds to the Internet. Soon so many sites dedicated to Nikola Tesla exploded with frantic chatter. The images spread across the world. "Eureka!" and "Finally!" popped up on the laptop screen again and again.

"The world will never be the same—you know that, don't you Emic?"

"I know, it will be better." She sat back now, lifting up her root beer, sipping it slowly, knowing that she had done the right thing.

eighteen

THE TIME HAD come to tell her father. Emic knew he would be asking about the auction again. He seemed to have forgiven her for everything, and she felt if she didn't deserve it while still knowing secrets.

"Grandpa was a spy. He was leaking secrets to the Russians," she blurted out, as she watched him working in his study, emptying out the last of the cardboard moving boxes and organizing his shelves full of books. His back was turned to her, and he stood there motionless for a split second too long.

"I know," he said, without turning.

"But how much did you know?" she asked. She needed to know everything!

"Only that. He never told me more. After he married my mother and they started a family, I guess he just wanted his new life to be different from the life he had led during the war.

"He was in love with a spy. Her real name was Nancy Wake but most folk called her Hélène except the enemy—the Nazis referred to her as the White Mouse. She became the most wanted person by the Gestapo during World War II. When Pop and Nancy parachuted into the south of France over Auvergne, her parachute got tangled in a tree and Grandpa saved her. He cut her down, saying that he 'hoped all trees could bear such beautiful fruit.' They fell in love, but she was already married to a wealthy Frenchman, a fellow named Henri, who had died earlier in the war. She wrote about it in one of her postcards to him. When the war ended, they drifted apart, married other people, stopped writing, but he kept the camera, as he had taken an entire roll of pictures with it, mostly of her—I guess he just didn't have the heart to develop it. She really was beautiful. Anyway, some 'black suits' came to see us, somebody from the government, someone who didn't want the pictures to get out—I don't know why—and they wanted the camera, the film, and all the pictures that Scottie developed. However, they didn't know that

Scottie made duplicates of all the pictures."

"We should put them in a scrapbook," her father joked. "Can I see the pictures?"

Emic pulled the manila envelope out from behind her back, and handed the black and white images to him. He smiled at the depictions of the lovely female spy, then stopped dead as he flipped to a photo of a strange, wingless flying machine. "He did it. He really built it. I thought he was just imagining it. He built Tesla's Flying Machine, after all."

"What? I thought it was just a design in the journal."

Her father looked confused. "Journal?"

"Grandpa kept a journal from when he was in New York. The military sent him there to see if the old guy was sharing his inventions with other governments, but Grandpa and Tesla became friends. Everything is written in a journal that he hid at the bottom of his old cigar box. And Grandpa gave me something else, when I used to visit him—Tesla's missing journal. He told me to keep it safe."

"Let me see the journal."

Emic retrieved the journal and handed it over to her father. He flipped through, with amazement on his face.

"He wasn't crazy—he really did know Tesla! I could never find his journal after he died. To tell you the truth, I doubted it even existed. The military discharged him a few years after the war, claiming he was insane."

"How did he meet Grandma Zelda?"

"He eventually picked up some factory work, building cars, and met mom at the plant where they worked in about 1963. I was born in '65. For years, Dad told us about these inventions that would change the world: flying machines that needed no wings, no fuel source, and a Tesla Generator that could run forever. He tried for years to build them in an old shed behind our house, every day that he wasn't working at the factory, but nothing ever worked, and people thought he just saw too much during the war and lost his mind. After my mother died, he stopped eating—kept saying he forgot—and worked all the time on these crazy inventions. He would talk to himself, repeating 'The obvious is invisible.' Finally, the state put him in the Manteno State Hospital: they called it a 'mental health center.'"

"So, this picture of the Flying Machine up in the air— it proves it works, that it was real and he built it when he was in the South of France?"

"Who are the men standing next to him?" Emic noticing them smiling. And the strange contraption hovered about six feet off the ground behind them.

"Maybe engineers, physicists, scientists he met overseas during World War II that helped him test out Tesla's theories?" was all he could guess.

"They made us take the camera down off the eBay site

before a bidder could win it, but they didn't know that most of the pictures were only of Nancy Wake: I think they were expecting something else, something much more valuable, like proof that the Flying Machine would fly! But we didn't turn those over to them, and Scottie cut them off the negatives, too. Anyway, they seemed disappointed, but we told them there wasn't anything else, and they said that this would be our compensation, and not to talk about our little meeting." Handing the check over to her father, she added, "We should give some of it to Dublin for helping me, right?" She answered it herself: "He really needs a new laptop. Besides, we have some more research to do."

Howard looked at the number, eyes widening with disbelief at the amount in his hands. "Em, ten thousand dollars?"

"That will be enough seed money for Celianna, won't it?"

"Yes, that will do, Emic. That will do."

As DUBLIN SHUT his locker, Emic leaned against the cool metal neighboring door and asked him how he was doing.

"Good, I'm good. It looks like we're going to be stickin' around for a while—my dad's getting some help, some therapy, so my mom and dad are going to try and work things out and put the war behind them."

"That's great." She pulled out a small pouch. "I have something for you, too." She had put five crisp one hundred dollar bills inside. "You earned this. If it wasn't for you, I never would have found out about my grandfather, and we wouldn't have the money from the camera."

Dublin lurched towards her, lifting her into the air, and spinning her around. Emic giggled, embarrassed, and fully aware that their classmates could see them making a scene. As he lowered her down, his mouth brushed against her cheek and he whispered "Thank you" in her ear.

"Um...so..." she stammered. "My dad's opening a restaurant in town. Do you like Italian?"

"Does spaghetti like meatballs?" he said.

They both laughed. As they walked together down the corridor Dede joined them, and they began talking about their adventures. Emic felt this wonderful sense of joy, knowing beyond doubt that she had new friends, that she had a new place in the world.

nineteen

HER FATHER WAS standing at the back of the restaurant, wearing his freshly pressed, new white apron, and the biggest grin ever on his face. The tables were already full of patrons, admiring the genuine Italian décor and handwritten menus. Mama was wearing her favorite green dress, and had even put on glossy pink lipstick for the occasion. There were fresh wildflowers on every table, candles lit in little mason jars, and baskets of fresh, warm bread being dropped off by busy waiters and waitresses in crisp white button-up shirts and black pants, and red aprons around their waists to hold their pens and order pads.

"*Chi mangia bene, mangia italiano,*" boomed her father from the back of the room, visiting a few tables to check in with customers and allowing them to admire the proud chef, who seemed to be a celebrity in this small town, making this new Italian restaurant "the only place to be" on its grand opening night.

"What does that mean?" Luna leaned over to ask Emic, who was sitting opposite her.

"Those who eat well, eat Italian." Emic smiled back at her, and Luna smiled at her mom. Carol's hair was growing in now, and there was color and fullness returning to her checks.

"I'm so glad we could be here," Luna said to everyone.

It was midsummer and everyone was wearing clothes for warm nights in a southern town: sundresses with spaghetti straps, light linen shirts, blue jeans, and flowery skirts. Louis Prima was playing over the speakers as people lined up, waiting for a table, while others laughed and drank glasses of sweet wine or Shirley Temples.

"Hey, is that Dublin?" Luna asked. She could see a tall boy at the entrance, looking around for someone. "You're right, he *is* cute! And tall."

Her mother nudged her but still smiled. "Luna, don't embarrass the girl."

"Yes, don't embarrass the girl," Emic said, referring to herself and signaling Dublin to come join them at their table.

"Hi, I'm Dublin." He outstretched his hand in a gentlemanly way. "My parents are coming in, they are just looking for parking. The lot is packed, you'd think this was the only spot in town." He paused for emphasis, striking a pose. "Oh yeah, it is!"

Dublin's mom and dad came in a moment later, holding hands, and joined the growing table.

"Where's Sheila?" Carol asked.

"She got pulled into the kitchen to help. Apparently, Howard is making a huge mess," said the waiter, who had overheard their conversation as he leaned over and delivered another basket of warm bread and a bowl of garlicky oil for dipping.

"Oh, I brought that part you asked for," Dublin said to Emic. "What do you need it for anyway?" Dublin revealed a large metal ring with deep ridges cut into it.

"It's part of the voltage regulator on a little project I'm working on."

"Project, huh? So now you're an inventor?"

Luna smiled and thought about this.

"Yes," Emic announced to everybody. She grinned at Luna. "I'm an inventor, and I'm going to change the world!"